TWO-WAY STREET

TWO–WAY

STREET

BY MARY BLAIR IMMEL

𝕭
THE BETHANY PRESS
St. Louis, Missouri

Copyright © 1965 by The Bethany Press

Library of Congress Catalog Card Number 64-23620

Distributed by Thomas C. Lothian, Melbourne,
Australia, and Auckland, New Zealand, and by
The G. R. Welch Company, Toronto, Canada

MANUFACTURED IN THE UNITED STATES OF AMERICA

Contents

1.

Big Girls Don't Cry

It was six-thirty in the morning. Ordinarily, Karen Beal would have snuggled deeper in the warm covers, glad that she didn't have to get up and go to school today. But even though she had long ago outgrown the childish tradition of arousing the entire family to inspect her stocking hung over the fireplace, Karen felt the restless anticipation of her sixteenth Christmas morning sweep over her. She could stay in bed no longer.

It was silly to get up so early, she told herself. There were no other sounds in the old frame house on Linden Street to indicate that anyone else was awake. Nevertheless, she slipped her feet into the ridiculously oversized fluffy blue slippers and put on a quilted robe of matching blue nylon. Automatically she smoothed the sheets, pulled up the covers and punched the pillow on her bed. As she was arranging the white chenille spread, her foot kicked against the box she had shoved beneath the bed only a few days ago. She stooped and pulled it out as she had done so many times lately.

Inside the flat green suit box lay three long-playing

phonograph records. She had paid some money down and put them on lay-away early last September. She had made the final payment for them only three days ago. It had taken the rest of her allowance. Jennie Simmons, her best friend, had been with her when she went to the record store.

"You sure live dangerously," Jennie had said. "I wouldn't have dared spend so much money on something I wasn't sure I'd ever be able to use."

Karen didn't admit even to Jennie that she felt much of that same uncertainty. Karen's self-confidence in the project had been further undermined on the very evening she brought the records home when she heard Mother and Dad engaged in another one of their frequent discussions about money. That was why Karen had put the records in the old suit box and hidden them under her bed. It didn't seem possible to Karen that her parents would buy the portable hi-fi record player she had wanted for so long.

It wasn't the most expensive portable in the store, she thought defensively. Karen had been careful to point that fact out to her parents at every opportunity for the past several months. She also assured them that she wouldn't expect any other presents for herself under the tree if she could just have the record player.

Now, in the early gray light of this Christmas morning, Karen said to herself, "Maybe I can sell these records to somebody else who can use them."

Karen moved aimlessly over to the window in the corner of her room and curled up on the small padded window seat. Her breath made a hazy design on the glass as she looked outside. There had been a light snow a few days ago, but it hadn't really been enough to cover the stubbly brown lawn. It wouldn't have made a very attractive Christmas card scene.

Karen shoved her hands deep into the large square pockets of her robe and unexpectedly touched a crumpled piece of paper. It was a telegram from her brother, Cliff, up at Northwood State College. Karen didn't have to look at the coarse yellow paper to recall exactly what the typed words said.

Cliff's telegram had arrived last night. Karen and her dad had been eating a rather haphazard supper in the kitchen. Mother was suffering from another of her migraine headaches and was lying on the living room couch with a damp, cold cloth covering her eyes. Dad had been late in getting home from work. Karen wasn't sure whether that was the cause of her mother's headache or not. Lately both her parents were tense and easily irritated.

Finally at seven o'clock that evening when it became obvious to Karen that her mother was not going to prepare dinner, Karen started some toasted cheese sandwiches. Not long after that, Dad came home. He didn't say much but sat down at the kitchen table which was unattractively decorated with mustard and pickle and mayonnaise jars.

When the telegram came, Mother evidently didn't hear the doorbell or simply didn't choose to answer it. The messenger boy pounded vigorously on the kitchen door.

"Didn't see no light in the front," the boy had said, looking through the screen door at them curiously.

For some reason, Karen felt ashamed of the cluttered kitchen table.

"I almost gave up till I saw the lights on back here," the boy continued as Dad signed for the telegram. "Always hate to miss people with a telegram. I like to give folks good service, 'specially on Christmas Eve."

Karen glanced at her dad. The corners of his mouth turned up a bit as he dug into his pocket for a tip to reward the hinting messenger.

"Well, merry Christmas to you and yours," said the boy as he clattered down the back steps.

"It's from Cliff," Dad had said when he tore the envelope open.

His eyes darted over the message and then he read it aloud, "CHANGE OF PLANS . . . CHRISTMAS AT GORDON'S . . . PRESENTS MAILED . . . HAPPY HOLIDAYS . . . CLIFF."

He handed the telegram to Karen. She looked at it, fighting tears. How could Cliff decide not to come home for Christmas? It wouldn't be anything at all without him. But, maybe he just couldn't face another holiday fiasco. Karen remembered dismally what it was like when he was home for Thanksgiving vacation. There was an argument over the size of the turkey and how much Mother paid for it. Dad left the house angrily and spent most of Thanksgiving Day at his office. When he didn't return by dinner time, Mother insisted on serving the meal regardless of his absence. She refused to let anyone call him and tell him the meal was ready. She said that he shouldn't walk out on his family on a special day. Then Mother went to her room. Karen and Cliff found themselves sitting down to the huge turkey dinner all by themselves. Dad had been right, Karen thought ironically, the turkey was too big—too big for just two people.

Maybe Cliff was lucky that he didn't have to come home here and be a part of the uncomfortable atmosphere that permeated this house. But, Karen thought, he could have at least considered her. Cliff should know that she would

10

have no choice than to spend Christmas here with just Mother and Dad.

Karen turned from the telegram and looked up at her dad. She wondered if he suspected what had been going on in her mind. So, Karen did the only thing she could think of to protect herself—to protect them all. Flippantly she made an exaggerated show of counting the words on the yellow paper.

"Say, the old holiday spirit really got into our big brother, didn't it? He used eleven words."

Her dad seemed relieved at this attempted humor and snorted, "His name doesn't count. He made it in ten words all right."

"Well," Karen said, and busied herself digging a reluctant pickle from the jar in the center of the table, "that's old thrifty Cliff for you."

When Karen looked up again, she saw her mother standing in the kitchen archway. Silently Karen handed her the telegram.

Her mother read it and then looked at Dad. Her lips pressed together in a thin line and without any make-up outlining them, her mouth seemed almost blue. She crumpled up the telegram and let it fall to the kitchen table.

"Perhaps it's for the best," Mother said, "considering the circumstances."

The telegram lay there on the kitchen table in front of them, like some grotesque centerpiece, as Karen and her dad finished their sandwiches silently.

Later that evening, when Karen went through the kitchen to put gifts for her parents under the tree in the living room, she saw the telegram still lying there on the table. She picked it up and started to throw it in the wastebasket, but for some unexplained reason, she put it into the pocket of her robe instead.

Now, this morning, as she sat by the window looking out at nothing in particular, Karen couldn't help but think that this was probably the dreariest Christmas she would ever spend.

Karen glanced at the funny little heart-shaped clock on her dresser. She remembered that the clock was something else she had wanted so badly she could hardly stand it. Things had seemed so happy and simple when she was a little girl. Perhaps things were not really that happy, though; she had been too young to be aware of what was happening. Surely, the estrangement of her parents couldn't have occurred suddenly. Something must have been festering all along that she just hadn't understood or recognized. Love between two people just couldn't shrivel up quickly like a piece of plastic that gets too near a flame.

She stared at the little clock as though willing it to get later quickly. At seven-fifteen it was still too early to be up on a holiday. Maybe the little clock was wrong. It didn't really keep good time anymore. Perhaps it was later.

She put on her old red plaid skirt and a matching red sweater. She wasn't going to be able to wear that outfit much longer, unless the fashion called for much shorter skirts, which hardly seemed possible.

Karen stood at the mirror of her dressing table and brushed her caramel-colored hair. It was just this year that she learned to stop fighting the thick, heavy waves. She accepted the fact that she'd probably never be able to force it into the latest styles, but at least it was shiny and had a natural wave. After she brushed it out, she managed to pull a tiny wisp of a curl down on her left temple.

She leaned forward and peered analytically at herself in the mirror.

"A face like a fox," she said in disgust. "I've got a face that is long and narrow and pointed like a scared little fox. If my eyes were brown instead of blue like Dad's, I'd really have to watch out for the horses and the hounds."

Even by attempting to dress leisurely, Karen managed to consume only half an hour. She wondered vaguely why she couldn't dress so quickly on a school morning.

Quarter till eight. All decent, respectable people should be up by now, she decided. She went into the kitchen and got out the cookbook. She wished she had thought to plan this breakfast ahead of time. She could have baked something special like an apple ring. As it was, she'd have to settle for biscuits. But then, Dad always said her biscuits were second only to Grandmother's.

As she floured the cutting board a sudden inspiration came to her and she dug through the bottom drawer of the cupboard for the cookie cutters. She picked out a fat Santa and a reindeer. She discarded them both and selected instead a Christmas tree. She smiled to herself as she cut the triangular doughy shapes and put them on the baking sheet. She would make this a festive day in spite of everything. Perhaps that was all this family needed—someone working actively to make them all happy again.

Karen set the timer on the oven as she slid the biscuits inside. She turned the ham that was slowly cooking on the back burner of the stove. She put a bright green tablecloth on the kitchen table. Her enthusiasm for the project spurred her creativity. She cut some pine branches from the back of the Christmas tree where it wouldn't show and placed them in the center of the table. Then she remembered a couple of old red candles and climbed up on the kitchen stepladder to get them from the top shelf of the cabinet. She stood back and observed her handiwork with pleasure.

Karen had just dished up the ham and started frying the eggs when her dad came into the kitchen.

"I thought maybe Indians were attacking the fort, judging by all the noise out here," he said.

"I'm glad you're here," Karen said, putting the pancake turner into his hand. "Will you please take care of these eggs while I call Mother?"

Karen poured a cup of hot coffee, put it on a tray, and carried it into the living room.

"Mother," she called softly. "Mother, here's some coffee."

Karen looked down at the woman who was lying on the couch. Her dark hair framed a small, delicately formed face. She opened her eyes slowly and if there had not been dark rings about them, they would have been lovely. Karen always wished that she had inherited her mother's large brown eyes with their long, dark lashes like bits of black lace. Karen couldn't help but think how vulnerable and sad her mother looked.

"Breakfast is ready, Mother," she said. "Merry Christmas."

Her mother sat up and took the coffee and drank it in swift gulps like someone who had just discovered an oasis on the desert. It made Karen's throat burn to think of that hot liquid but her mother didn't seem to be affected by the scalding temperatures. Karen helped her slip into her flowered housecoat, and they went into the kitchen.

"Now, you two sit down here and let me wait on you," Karen ordered.

"Here's some strawberry jam to decorate your Christmas

trees," she said, placing the dish in the center of the table. Her voice sounded absurd as she attempted to inject some gaiety into the morning.

Dad ate with obvious pleasure but Mother did little more than make a token effort to nibble at the food on her plate. Karen would have given almost anything if she could revive the old sparkle that used to be there.

"Look," she said. "I know we're all just dying to wash up the dishes, but I can't wait to see our presents."

Mother had a vague look on her face as though she had been recalled from some distant place to which no one else had access.

"The presents? Oh, yes, I guess we ought to see them. I do have some last-minute things to do."

Karen got up and started returning the butter and salt and pepper to the cupboard. She could hear Mother and Dad talking together in the living room.

"Where did you put it?" her mother was asking.

"It's in the trunk of the car. I thought that would be the best place to hide it."

"Did you ask them to gift wrap it at the store?" Mother inquired.

"No, I didn't think about that. Haven't we got some paper around the house?" Dad asked.

"It's too late for that now," Mother said querulously. "She'll just have to get it in the box."

"Somehow that doesn't seem very Christmas-like."

"No, nothing about it has been much like Christmas ought to be, has it?" her mother accused.

"Please, let's not start anything now. Could we have just one day without an argument?"

Karen felt resentment welling up inside of her. She

wished she could shut out the sound of the dissension that was threatening to spoil the occasion.

Her dad called, "We're ready now."

Karen went into the living room. Her determination to enjoy the day was waning.

"Why don't you open this first?" her dad suggested. "I'm sorry we didn't have time to get it wrapped."

Karen was provoked at herself for not feeling a thrill of excitement when she saw the large cardboard carton and realized that it contained the hi-fi set. Now she could use the records after all. She ought to be the happiest girl in the world.

She tried to act enthusiastic. She knelt and began tugging at the strips of brown stick tape which sealed the box lid.

"It's just what I wanted," she said, but the words sounded brittle and phony. "It's just wonderful."

Her dad said apologetically, "I see we didn't think this out very well. We neglected to get you any records to play on it. You'll have to wait until after Christmas when the stores open."

Karen felt a bit sheepish as she admitted, "I hoped this would be what you'd get me. I bought some records. I have them in my room."

"Well, then, everything is just fine, isn't it?" her dad said.

Karen nodded. She reached under the tree and got two presents. She handed one to each of her parents.

"Here," she said. "I hope you like these things."

Her dad removed the blue tissue paper which covered his gift. He examined the plastic box containing a variety of nylon twine and tiny colored feathers. "A fly-tying out-fit. How about that? This will sure come in handy when I go fishing."

Karen wished he would take time to go out to the lake once in a while. His real estate business kept him so involved lately that he hardly ever took a day off.

"Hurry, Mother," Karen urged. "Open your present and see what it is."

Her mother's fingers worked slowly as she unfastened the large red satin bow.

"I made it in clothing class. I hope it fits."

Her mother held up a white lace blouse. "It's lovely, Karen. It really is."

Karen looked hopefully at her dad. When she was making the blouse, Karen thought how pretty Mother would look in it. It was the kind of blouse to wear some place very special, not just to wear while she worked at Dad's office. Wouldn't it be wonderful if Dad would offer to take them out to dinner tonight? But Dad didn't seem to notice the blouse, as he sat turning the plastic fly box over and over in his hands.

There were a few more gifts under the tree. There was a royal blue skirt and sweater set from her mother. There was a book from her dad. Karen kept trying to work up enthusiasm for the other little things she had purchased for them. A bracelet and some perfume for Mother. Ties and shaving lotion for Dad.

There were several presents from Grandmother Newsome, the only grandparent Karen had. The rest of the packages under the tree were for Cliff.

Dad and Mother didn't exchange any presents with each other.

The whole business of opening gifts had consumed only forty-five awkward minutes. Mother got up and began to gather wrappings from the floor. Karen noticed that this year Mother didn't sort out the best ribbons and paper to save. Instead she simply wadded everything in a ball and threw it into the trash. Then she went back to her room and closed the door.

"I'm going out and straighten up my work bench," Dad said, and went to the garage.

Karen took the new record player and put it on the kitchen table. She got the records out from under her bed and stacked them on the automatic changer. As the first record fell into place and the needle slipped into the groove, she looked at the pile of dirty breakfast dishes. Someone had to do them.

Karen stood at the sink with her hands in the soapy, hot water, feeling the equally hot tears behind her eyes when she heard the Elder Brothers swing into their mellow version of "Big Girls Don't Cry."

"How appropriate," she scolded herself. "I got everything I thought I wanted for Christmas. What am I blubbering about?"

The song was almost over when the telephone rang. Karen dried her hands and hurried to pick up the receiver. It was Jennie Simmons.

"Hi, Karen. Did you get it?" her friend asked.

"Get what?" Karen asked dumbly.

"Get what!" Jennie exclaimed. "The record player, silly. The thing you've done nothing but talk about for the last four months."

"Oh, yes. I got it. I was just playing some records."

"I can't wait to hear it," Jennie hinted.

Karen knew Jennie was waiting for an invitation, but she couldn't bear to invite Jennie to the house.

She paused for a moment and then said, "Jennie, I wish I could ask you to come over but—Mother isn't feeling too well today."

"That's too bad," Jennie said sympathetically. "I wondered why you sounded so—so quiet. I suppose you have to stay there and take care of her."

"No, not really," Karen said. "I think she'd rather be alone. She has a headache."

"Do you think you could come over?" Jennie asked. "It's pretty noisy here but I guess we could turn up the record player loud enough for us to hear it."

In the background Karen could hear laughing and whooping at the Simmons' house. Suddenly she felt that if she could be with Jennie, the day wouldn't be a total loss.

"I'm sure no one will care if I leave," Karen said. "Maybe I can get Dad to drive me over to your house. It's too far to walk with this hi-fi set."

"I'll tell you what," Jennie offered. "Gary is home and he's been itching to get his hands on the car. I'll have him come and pick you up. See you in about half an hour."

"Sure thing," Karen said and placed the receiver back in its cradle. She took a deep breath. Gary is home! She had almost forgotten that he would be home for the college holiday when Cliff didn't show up.

Karen told herself to relax. There was no reason to be hopeful that Gary would pay any more attention to her now than he ever had. Karen was his younger sister's best friend and that was that!

Karen hurriedly washed the rest of the dishes and left them to drain in the rack. She dashed to her room and pulled off the old red skirt and sweater. She put on the new blue outfit Mother had given her. She breathed a sigh of relief. It was the right size. She looked in the mirror a bit self-consciously, knowing that the brilliant blue skirt and sweater emphasized the color of her eyes.

At the door of Mother's room, she called softly, but

there was no answer. She knocked but go no response. She went out to the garage where her dad was cleaning out his tool box.

"Dad, Jennie Simmons wants me to come over to her house."

He started to say something and then shrugged.

"I thought it might be best to play my new records over at the Simmons' place. That way I won't disturb Mother."

"I guess you're right," Dad said in a resigned tone. "Come in at a reasonable hour."

Karen hurried back to the desk in the living room and wrote a note to Mother and slipped it under the bedroom door.

Quickly she wiped the dust from the new records and slipped them into their cardboard carton. She was trying to figure out just what she could say to Gary when she heard the knock on the front door and rushed to open it.

She was surprised to see a broad-shouldered boy with closecut red hair standing there. It was Marty Riffner, staring at her with his perpetually sardonic grin.

Marty never failed to irritate her in journalism class at school. As editor of their weekly newspaper, he openly scorned the talents of any female and he seemed especially critical of her. He annoyed her even more when it came to the subject of Gary Simmons. Marty had figured out long ago that Karen was interested in Jennie's older brother.

"Riffner and Simmons at your service," he said jauntily.

Karen was certain he had detected her disappointment at not seeing Gary at the door.

He added, "He's out in the car and if you're a good girl, I'll arrange it so you can sit next to him."

Karen choked back an angry reply. She slipped into her

coat and hurried down the front walk, leaving Marty to carry the record player.

WHEN they arrived at the Simmons' place, Jennie was waiting and swung open the door. As Karen stepped inside, she heard a shrill scream and felt a rubber-tipped arrow fly past her head. From behind a chair dashed ten-year-old Joey Simmons. He was dressed in an elaborate feathered headdress. The front room carpet was strewn with tiny dresses and coats and doll furniture belonging to two identical Barbie dolls.

"This is the penalty for having twin sisters," Jennie commented as she cleared a path through the scattered doll clothes. She held up a tiny dress and said, "Have you ever tried to sew for anyone with a one-and-a-half-inch waist?"

Jennie paused for a moment while she vainly tried to stop an argument between the eight-year-old girls about which doll belonged to whom.

"Let's go in the dining room," Karen suggested. "We could set up the record player in there."

"Ha," Jennie said. "If you think it's bad in here where the kids are, just wait until you see what's happening in there."

Seated at the dining room table were Jennie's parents, eating popcorn and howling with laughter as they maneuvered brightly colored plastic disks about a large maze.

The over-crowded, gift-strewn, child-filled house seemed to vibrate with laughter. Karen couldn't help but think it was the most wonderful place she had ever been, especially when she compared it to the dismal atmosphere she had left at home.

Soon Jennie and Karen and even Marty and Gary found places around the dining room table. Karen lost track of

21

how long they played the crazy game, but it seemed to get more boisterous as the day wore on. Finally, Mrs. Simmons held up her hands and said, "I've got to stop now or we'll never have dinner. Karen and Marty, you'll both stay, won't you?"

Within a matter of minutes, Mrs. Simmons had assigned everyone a job.

Everyone began dashing about bumping into everyone else. Somehow out of all the confusion a beautifully set table, complete with tall green candles and a pot of miniature poinsettias, emerged from the chaos. And Karen found herself seated between Gary and Marty.

"Let's hold hands around the table as we have our prayer," Mrs. Simmons suggested. "Somehow it feels good to enclose the family circle this way."

Karen felt Gary's strong hand close over her fingers. She bowed her head and listened to Mr. Simmons' voice thanking God for the food and the season and asking that they be led to show their gratitude by the way they lived.

Karen realized as she listened that it had been a long time since she and her family had paused for a blessing. Mealtimes had been tense and strained—a mere necessity to sustain life. Maybe if they could just get together in prayer, things would change between Mother and Dad.

As soon as Mr. Simmons said, "Amen," ten-year-old Joey piped up, "I know why Momma always likes to have us hold hands. That way everybody gets an equal chance to grab the food when the blessing is over."

"No one needs to do any grabbing today," Mrs. Simmons assured them. "There's more than enough for everybody."

After dinner the assembly line swung into action. Mr. Simmons and the boys cleared the table while Mrs. Simmons washed the dishes. Jennie and Karen dried and Rosemary and Rebecca put plates and glasses away.

When they were finished, the children scrambled about picking up their gifts and putting them away. Mr. Simmons added another huge log to the fire. Gary went to his room and came back with a guitar.

"I didn't know you played the guitar," Karen said, surprised.

"I don't really play," Gary admitted. "I just do a little chording. My roommate up at school is teaching me."

His fingers found the proper position on the frets and he began to strum the strings gently. They all listened as he played a brief introduction and then started the chords of "Silent Night." Little by little they joined in singing. Mrs. Simmons had a high, thin but sweet voice, and Mr. Simmons' deep baritone filled in the empty spots. They sang all the Christmas carols they could think of. Then Gary taught them some folk songs he had learned at college.

When they ran out of songs and breath, Mrs. Simmons got up and switched on a table lamp.

"I'll get the dessert now before these children go to sleep," she said. "They were up at the crack of dawn this morning."

"Karen," Jennie said. "Why don't you put on your records now. We can dance." She turned to Marty who was sprawled out in front of the fire. "Come on, lazy," she said. "You need some exercise if you're going to eat any cake and ice cream."

Karen adjusted the volume on the record player and turned back to the fire. She started to sit down when Gary said, "Shall we join the party?"

It was the first time Karen had ever danced with Gary.

She ignored the fact that he probably had asked her out of courtesy because Jennie and Marty were dancing.

It was almost ten o'clock that evening when Mr. Simmons said, "I think we'd better be getting you home, Karen. Your folks will think we have kidnapped you."

"I'll drive her home," Gary volunteered.

Karen braced herself, expecting Marty to horn in. Surprisingly he said he'd better be getting home himself and he left.

Karen and Gary drove through the quiet streets. A damp snow had begun to cover the town with a white veneer.

Karen wanted to say several things, but most of her thoughts seemed like dialogue out of a third-rate movie.

"Thanks so much for bringing me home, Gary. It's been a wonderful day."

"It was fun, wasn't it?" he agreed.

Just then Karen saw the porch light flicker on.

"Is that a gentle hint from the powers that be?" Gary asked.

Karen was trying to think up some sort of an answer to prolong the conversation when the front door opened, and Dad came out carrying a small suitcase.

"Looks like your father is going somewhere," Gary said.

Karen was stunned.

"Maybe he was called out of town on business," Gary suggested. "Tough break right at Christmastime."

Karen clutched desperately at the straw. "Yes, that must be it, a business trip," she said unconvincingly.

"If you hurry, you can catch up with him and say 'good-by.' "

Karen fumbled with the handle of the car door but Gary had already come around to help her out.

"I'll take your records and the hi-fi up on the porch for you," he said.

"Thanks," Karen called and hurried toward her dad.

He rolled down the window just enough to let the sound of his voice fill the calm night air.

"Go into the house, Karen. It's cold out here."

"But, Dad, where are you going? When are you coming back?" She spoke in a whisper, hoping he would reply the same way. However, his voice was strident and loud.

"Ask your mother. She's got all the answers," he snapped and backed the car out of the driveway.

Karen was hurt and angry. She knew Gary had witnessed the entire scene. She walked slowly up on the front porch.

"Can you carry all of this inside without help?" he asked.

"Yes, I can handle it. Thank you," she choked.

They stood awkwardly for a moment on the porch.

"I'm glad you spent Christmas with us," he said. "Maybe I'll see you before I have to go back to Northwood."

Karen watched him go down the front walk and get into the car. Tears of rage pushed their way from under her lids as she went into the house. She was glad it was dark and that her mother was in her room with the door closed. Karen didn't want to talk to anyone. Mother and Dad had had another fight, and this time Dad had left for good.

2.

Karen's Desperate Day

KAREN had a miserable night, falling into a deep, heavy sleep where she dreamed of the large box her record player had come in. The two figures that hovered over the box as they presented it to her were merely indistinct dark blobs, but she sensed they were Mother and Dad. In her dream she opened the box. The record player was not inside. Instead she saw Gary. As he reached out his hand to her, the two figures snatched the box away quickly. Karen woke up with a shaken feeling.

She got up and put on her blue robe. She went into the bathroom and splashed her face with cold water to drive away the sickening memory of the dreams.

When she went back to her bedroom and looked at the little heart-shaped clock on her night stand, she was amazed to find that she had almost slept the clock around. It was nearly ten in the morning.

She went into the kitchen. It was really too late for breakfast and too early for lunch. She stood in the center of the kitchen and listened. There was no other sound than her own breathing in the quiet house. She went to the door of her mother's room and stood listening for a moment. There was no noise from inside the room.

Karen tapped softly on the door. "Mother," she called. "Mother, are you there?"

There was no reply, no indication of any movement inside. Karen felt a brief moment of fear, and then she calmed herself by the realization that Mother might have gone to work. Maybe she and Dad had been able to settle their disagreements, and Mother was back at her desk in Beal's Real Estate Agency. Karen turned the knob of her mother's door.

Mother was there. She lay so quietly on the bed in the darkened room that Karen's heart pushed its way up to the back of her throat and threatened to strangle her.

"Mother, are you all right?" Karen cried out.

Her mother did not move. Karen hurried to the bed and shook her mother by the shoulders. Slowly her eyes fluttered open.

"Mother," Karen all but shouted with relief. "Mother, I thought you were . . ."

"What time is it?" her mother asked thickly.

"It's almost ten in the morning," Karen answered, raising the window shades to let some light into the room. "I'll get you some coffee."

Mother closed her eyes again, and didn't answer. Karen looked about the bedroom. On the dresser was a small bottle of pills. It was three-quarters full. Karen was sure they were the pills the doctor had prescribed to ease her mother's tension and help her relax. She snapped the plastic cap on the top of the bottle and slipped it into the pocket of her robe. Perhaps she was being overdramatic, but accidents sometimes happened.

Karen hurried to the kitchen and put the coffee pot on the back burner of the stove. She also started to boil some water to make oatmeal.

When the coffee and oatmeal were ready, she helped Mother sit up against a pile of pillows at her back.

"I'm not really hungry," her mother kept repeating.

"You haven't eaten much of anything lately," Karen coaxed. "You're going to be ill if you keep this up."

Karen sat on the edge of the bed and urged her mother to take a few swallows of oatmeal.

"Do you know what this reminds me of?" Karen said in an effort to divert her mother's attention and keep her awake. "Remember the time you and Cliff and I started to drive to Grandmother's house one March? We ran into a blizzard on the way, and the car broke down."

Karen watched her mother's face change slowly. It was the first time in days she had seemed interested in anything.

"I remember we got terribly cold out in the snow," her mother said. "We walked and walked until we discovered an old farmhouse. It wasn't a fancy place, but they invited us in and were so very kind to us. I remember the old farm woman. When she saw us, she kept saying, 'What in the world are you doing out in a storm like this with those two little babies?'"

Karen laughed. "I was really insulted that she'd called me a baby. I thought I was pretty big then."

"You must have been about four years old," Mother said. "Cliff would have been eight at the time. I'm surprised you can remember that."

"I remember that the woman made us take scalding hot baths."

"Yes, her husband had to heat the water on the stove. It was lucky they had an indoor pump."

"She gave you one of her flannel nightgowns," Karen added. "It looked like a tent on you."

Karen looked at her mother. Some color had come back into her cheeks. Her eyes seemed to acquire some luster, as though she were finally looking at the world rather than staring at a glazed surface.

"That was the time I almost took my first train ride," Karen said, pleased that her mother was willing to talk and reminisce. "You arranged to have a mechanic tow the car to a garage to be repaired. We were going to go home on the train, but Dad borrowed a car and came to get us. He thought he was doing us a big favor by coming, but I was disappointed not to get to ride on the train."

Her mother sighed. "I just remember how relieved I was to get started for home again."

"We've had some happy times together as a family, Mother," Karen said hopefully. "Maybe it could be like that again."

When Mother looked at her, Karen saw that her eyes were bright with tears. "Sometimes people just can't go on trying to make unpleasant things turn out happily, Karen," she said, and her voice sounded very weary. "Sometimes the energy for that sort of living fades away."

It was obvious she didn't want to continue the conversation.

"I'll clear away these dishes," Karen said, picking up the tray.

Karen put the dishes on the drainboard and tried to decide what to do next. She had imagined for a while that there was going to be a change in Mother's attitude. She didn't want to believe that the conflict between Mother and Dad could not be worked out.

"Karen, have you seen my medicine?" Mother called from the other room.

Karen's hand dipped instinctively into the pocket of her robe and closed over the small bottle of pills. She didn't answer her mother but went into the bathroom and closed the door. She could hear her mother moving through the house, opening and closing cupboard doors and saying, "It's got to be here somewhere."

Karen felt cold all over. She didn't know exactly what she should do. She didn't want to withhold the pills from her mother, and yet she was afraid of what her mother might do out of desperation. Mother seemed to spend too much time seeking relief from her headaches by sleeping. It couldn't be good for her. It wasn't solving any problems. Karen bit her lower lip thoughtfully, and then opened the medicine bottle. She shook out all but two of the tablets. On second thought, she decided it would appear less suspicious to her mother if there were more than two, so she added three more. Even if her mother took them all at once, so few might not harm her. Karen flushed the remaining pills away.

"I think I've found what you're looking for," she called. "Why don't you lie down, and I'll bring your medicine to you with some water."

She drew a glass of cold water from the tap and took it to Mother. She held out one pill in her hand.

"I checked the label. You may have one pill now, and if you should need another, you may take it in four more hours."

Mother swallowed the pill and held out her hand for the bottle.

"I checked the instructions on the bottle," Karen said

emphatically. "You shouldn't need another tablet for four hours. I'll watch the clock and bring it to you then."

"Give me the medicine," her mother demanded.

Karen had never been able to disobey her mother. She handed her the bottle. Mother took it and went back to her room.

Karen stood and looked at the telephone on the small table near the window. She wondered whether or not to call Dad at his office. She decided to wait.

Karen went to her room and put on a pair of brown woolen slacks with a white long-sleeved blouse. She tied a gold and yellow and orange silk scarf at her neck. She brushed her hair until it crackled with electricity. As she added a touch of lipstick, she hoped vaguely that perhaps Gary would come over. He had said he might see her before he went back to college, but perhaps he was just being polite.

Leisurely she made up her bed and straightened her room. She had to do something to keep from worrying about her mother and the other problems that nagged her. At last she decided to dismantle the Christmas tree. There was no use to leave it standing. Christmas was definitely over at the Beal house.

She was getting the vacuum cleaner out of the closet preparing to clean the pine needles from the carpet, when she heard the door to her mother's room open.

"Karen, I need you," her mother called in a voice that sounded strange and fuzzy. "Karen, I'm out of medicine. I want you to go to the drugstore and get a refill of this prescription for me. Have you seen my purse?"

"You ought to have some pills left," Karen said, feeling frightened. "You weren't supposed to take one for another hour yet."

"I took them all. I had to sleep. The doctor didn't prescribe the right dosage."

"Why don't I make some more coffee? We could have soup and a sandwich. You'll feel better after you eat some lunch," Karen offered.

"Karen," her mother's voice sliced through the air with a jagged edge. "Don't argue with me. My nerves just won't take any more."

Karen took the empty pill bottle which her mother thrust into her hand. There was no advantage in arguing with her. When Mother went back to her room and shut the door, Karen quickly picked up the telephone receiver and dialed Dad's office. Maybe he could tell her what to do. Mother shouldn't have any more of that medicine. Karen listened as the dull buzz on the other end of the line sounded in the ear piece. Where could he be? She needed help!

Karen was aware of a strange sound in the lonely house. She realized it was coming from her mother's room. She went to the door and listened. It was a series of low moans, the kind of sobs Karen had never heard from a human being before. It sounded as though they were being torn forcibly from deep inside her mother's throat. Karen was deeply agitated. She ran from the house, her hands squeezed into tight fists. She had run several blocks before she stopped to catch her breath. When she did rest, she realized it was beginning to snow again.

SHE walked briskly toward the shopping center near the high school where there was a drugstore. She bent her head against the blowing snow and wished that she had taken time to get her scarf and gloves.

When she got to the drugstore and pushed open the glass

doors, a wave of warmth and noise greeted her. Almost every booth was filled with high school kids laughing and talking. The juke box in the corner was blaring out, "Laugh, Baby, Laugh." Several kids were dancing, and others were snapping their fingers in time to the music.

She brushed the snow from her face and out of her hair.

"Hi, Karen," called a voice from a booth.

Her heart gave a strange little twist and flip-flopped as she recognized it.

"Hello, Gary," she said and hoped that the warm feeling which crept up her neck into her hairline didn't mean that she was blushing furiously.

"You look cold," he said. "Can I buy you some hot chocolate?"

She would have given anything to stop and sit with him while they drank hot chocolate, but the memory of her mother's distress made her say, "Thanks anyway, Gary. I wish I could, but I've got to get a prescription filled for my mother and get home with it."

"You could drink it while you're waiting for the druggist to make up your order," he said. "I've got the car outside. I can drive you home in a minute."

Karen nodded. Gary went to the counter to place the order as she went to the pharmacy at the back of the store.

She handed the small bottle to the man behind the high desk.

"I'd like to get a refill on this prescription for my mother," Karen said.

The man slipped a pair of half-lensed eyeglasses on his nose and peered at the bottle for a minute and then looked down at her. Karen thought he had a strange expression on his face.

"The date on this bottle is December 23," he said. "If

these pills were taken as prescribed there should be more left."

Karen thought guiltily about the pills she had flushed down the toilet.

"Well, she, ah, . . ." Karen hesitated while she tried to think. "Well, somehow some of the pills got lost. She can't find them."

As soon as Karen had said it, she realized how contrived it sounded.

"I'm sorry, young lady," the druggist said, removing his glasses and leaning toward her. "This medicine is pretty strong stuff, and I can't possibly give you a refill without a doctor's order."

"But Mother is so sick," Karen begged.

"You'll have to talk to your doctor," he said firmly.

Karen saw Gary coming toward her carrying a mug of steaming hot chocolate.

"All right," Karen said, reaching for the bottle, but the druggist held it out of her reach.

"I'll just keep this here until you come back," he said.

Karen's face burned. She felt like a criminal.

"Here's your cocoa," Gary said, putting the mug in her hands. "This will warm you up. You look kind of pale. Are you all right?"

"I'm fine," she said weakly. She took a drink of the scalding liquid and burned her tongue.

"I think all the booths are filled," he said. "Would you like to sit at the counter?"

"No," Karen said. "Gary, I really ought to be getting home in a hurry."

"I'm sorry about your mother," Gary said. "Is it anything serious?"

"No," she said. "I mean, I'm not sure. She . . . well, she has a lot of headaches and can't sleep. She's so miserable."

She wondered frantically what she was going to do. Mother obviously needed the medicine. Karen was afraid she had been wrong to destroy the pills, but she just couldn't let her mother take an overdose.

"Gary," she said, handing him back the mug of cocoa. "It was swell of you to get this for me, but it's so hot I can't drink it now. I need to get back to Mother."

"Sure," he said. "I'll take you home."

He hurried over to the counter and returned with the cocoa in a paper carton. "Here, now you can take it with you and drink it on the way as it cools."

He took her arm, and they threaded their way through the roomful of dancing kids. When they were outside, he opened the car door, and she got inside. It took a moment for the motor to turn over, for it was cold.

Gary drove out of the parking lot and turned down Linden Street.

When they were a few blocks from her house, Karen said suddenly, "Gary, will you think I'm an awful idiot if I ask you to turn around and drive me downtown instead of taking me home?"

"Where to?" he asked, turning the corner.

"Do you know where my dad's office is? I need to talk to him. I'm worried about my mother."

Gary stopped the car in front of a small brick building where a sign in the window announced, "GLEN BEAL, REAL ESTATE—NOTARY PUBLIC."

Karen went to the door of the office. She turned the knob. It didn't yield. She pushed at the door, but it wouldn't open.

"I don't see any lights," Gary said.

Karen knocked loudly on the glass door until it rattled

35

threateningly. "Maybe he's in the back room and can't hear me."

"But wouldn't he leave the door open if he were in there?" Gary asked reasonably.

Karen stopped pounding at the door. "I guess you're right," she said, not knowing what to do next.

Karen remembered that Gary had been with her last night when Dad had left the house with his suitcase. It would have been so good to confide how worried she was, how frightened and hurt, how helpless she felt, but Karen decided against it. She was certain he'd be as sympathetic as any friend would be, but Karen didn't want Gary as a casual friend who would feel sorry for her. She also remembered the suggestion which Gary had made last night about her dad going out of town. She heard herself saying hollowly, "Maybe Dad hasn't come back to town yet from his business trip. I thought he'd have returned to his office by now."

As soon as she said it, she hated herself for trying to cover up in such a dishonest way.

"Karen," Gary suggested, "why don't we drop by my house and get my mom? She'd be glad to go over and help look after your mother until your dad gets home. She'll know what to do."

"Oh, no," Karen stammered, thinking of her mother lying back in the dark bedroom crying in her anguish. She couldn't bear to have Mrs. Simmons see her mother like that. "Thanks, but everything will be okay. I'm sure Dad will be home by this evening."

Karen turned back to Gary's car. "I do think I'd better get home now."

As Gary left her at her house, he said, "I really meant what I said, Karen. If you need anything, please call."

"Thank you, Gary," she said, gratefully, wanting to say so much more, but not daring to. She went into the house.

"Karen, where have you been?" her mother called as soon as Karen opened the door. "My head is splitting wide open. Where is the medicine?"

"I couldn't get it," Karen said fearfully. "The druggist wouldn't refill the prescription without the doctor's approval."

Her mother covered her eyes with her hands and cried desperately, "What am I going to do?"

"Why don't I call Dr. Smyzer and see what he says?"

Her mother agreed helplessly and went back to lie down.

Karen rubbed her cold hands together and then thumbed through the phone directory. She located the number and dialed it.

"Good afternoon, Dr. Smyzer's office," said an efficient voice at the other end of the line.

"This is Karen Beal. I'm calling about my mother. She's very ill, and I need to speak to Dr. Smyzer, please."

"I'm sorry," said the voice. "Dr. Smyzer is out on an emergency call right now. May I take a message?"

"My mother is having terrible headaches," Karen said, and then covered the mouthpiece as Mother called to her from the other room.

"Tell him I'm terribly nauseated. I'm so nervous I could scream."

Karen repeated the information and then said, "I think she's kind of hysterical now. She's been crying a lot. She used up the medicine the doctor gave her to help her relax."

Karen couldn't ignore the twinge of conscience she felt as she thought about the pills she had disposed of.

"The druggist wouldn't give me a refill without the doctor's approval," she said.

"I'll look at the records and see if I can authorize it for you," the voice seemed sympathetic.

"What did the doctor say?" her mother called again.

Once more Karen covered the mouthpiece. "The doctor isn't there. I'm talking to the nurse."

"Hello, Miss Beal," said the nurse. "I can't authorize a refill for you, but I'll try to locate the doctor and have him stop by your house."

"Thank you," Karen said.

"It does seem strange," the nurse continued. "Mrs. Beal should have more of that medication left."

"We'll wait for Dr. Smyzer to come," Karen said, eager to end the incriminating conversation.

Karen replaced the receiver and went to the door of her mother's room. "The doctor will come as quickly as he can."

"What am I going to do?" her mother groaned again and again.

Karen began to feel a truant sense of annoyance. She had done her best. Why didn't Mother try to help herself? Why couldn't she control herself?

"I'm going to make some soup," Karen said.

"I can't eat," her mother cried. "My stomach is still upset. Just let me alone until the doctor comes."

Karen closed the door to her mother's room. She couldn't stand to hear her like that. Karen returned to the telephone. She dialed Dad's number once more. She listened futilely as the buzz repeated its message that no one was there to help her. Why didn't Dad answer? Karen was just about to hang up when she heard a click, followed by her dad's voice.

"Real Estate. Glen Beal speaking."

"Oh, Dad," Karen said, almost collapsing with relief. "I've called and called you today. I came by the office and I couldn't find you anywhere."

"I was out showing a client some property," he said. "What do you want?"

"Mother's sick again, worse than she's ever been. I don't know what to do."

"What's the matter with her this time?" he asked flatly.

"It's another headache, and she's sick to her stomach. She starts crying and she can't stop. It's awful."

"Aren't those pills helping any?" Dad inquired.

"Oh, Daddy," Karen wailed. "Daddy, I'm afraid I've made a terrible mess of things, but I didn't know what else to do. When I woke her up this morning, she was so groggy it scared me. I was afraid she would take an overdose and maybe . . ." Karen couldn't express the fears she had felt. They sounded unrealistic now. "Well, I took most of the pills out of the bottle and got rid of them. I saved five, but she took all of them when she should have taken only two. She tried to get the prescription refilled, but the druggist wouldn't do it without the doctor's permission."

"Slow down, Karen, and let me get all of this straight," he said.

"She wants more pills, Dad. She just keeps moaning and crying. It scares me. Dad, can't you please come home now?"

There was a long silence on the other end of the line. Then he said, "Karen, I'm not coming home any more. Didn't your mother tell you?"

"Dad, you don't mean that!"

"Karen, you're a big girl now. Don't make this any harder than it already is."

"But I need you. I can't handle Mother. Please come home and talk to her."

"Right now there is nothing I can do or say that will

make any difference to your mother. I suppose I'm part of the reason she's ill."

"Where are you going to stay?" Karen asked.

"Right now I'm sleeping in the back room of the office. Eventually I'll have to get a room somewhere. I've neglected the business so long I can't even take time to look for a room. That's a switch, isn't it? I'm a real estate man who can't even find a home for himself."

"But, Dad," she protested. She felt in her pocket to find a handkerchief to stop the flood of tears that had come.

"Things are bad enough right now. Please don't cry. You're just making it worse for everybody," he said.

"Tell me what to do," she pleaded.

"Call your grandmother. She'll come. She'll know what to do."

Karen heard the click on the other end of the wire. She stood stunned and shocked. She put the dead receiver down. She felt as thought her dad had deserted her when she needed him most.

Alone in the empty house, she listened to the frightening sounds of her mother sobbing in the other room. Karen stared out of the window, watching the pale winter day shrink away into darkness. Every time a car passed by, Karen whispered, "Let it be him. Please let Dr. Smyzer come."

When she saw the doctor walking up the front steps at last, Karen was exhausted from the effort of her vigil.

Dr. Smyzer went right in to see Mother. Karen wandered purposelessly about the living room, straightening magazines that didn't need straightening.

Dr. Smyzer came quietly into the living room and said, "I gave your mother a sedative to relax her. She was extremely distraught. I couldn't make much sense out of her conversation. Where's your father? I'd better talk to him."

"Dad isn't here," Karen said.

"When do you expect him?"

Karen looked at the tall man with the shaggy white hair. He had been their doctor for a long time. His air of self-confidence reassured Karen. She had to confide in someone.

"Dr. Smyzer, my dad won't be home any more. He and Mother aren't getting along very well."

The old doctor nodded. "I suspected this was coming." He took off his glasses and rubbed his eyes. "Have you been here with your mother all day?"

Karen nodded.

"Then I want you to tell me everything you can think of that has happened." He paused. "First, could you get me a cup of coffee?"

Dr. Smyzer dumped two heaping spoonfuls of sugar into his cup as he listened to Karen.

He leaned his bulky form back in the chair and said, "I think the best thing for your mother now is to get her into the hospital where I can really look after her."

"What's wrong with her?"

"I think you can figure most of it out," he said. "I suppose the easiest way to explain it is by saying that her problems have simply become too much for her."

"Do you mean this is all in her mind?" Karen asked in surprise.

"If you mean that she just imagines that she's ill, the answer is no. The pain she is suffering is very real. It's driving her almost to distraction, but her illness is not caused by any organic disturbance. There's no disease. She does need rest in an atmosphere away from the things that seem to her to be insurmountable problems. I want her in a pri-

41

vate room where she doesn't have to see or talk to anyone or make any decisions for a while."

Dr. Smyzer poured himself another cup of coffee. "When does Cliff have to go back to school?"

"Cliff didn't come home for Christmas," Karen said. "I guess he didn't want to have to be involved in this kind of mess."

Dr. Smyzer nodded. "A thing like this gets to the whole family, doesn't it? You've had a rough go of it yourself, young lady. Do you want me to leave something here to settle your nerves?"

Karen shook her head. She was never going to be dependent on medicine to solve her problems if she could help it. "I'll be all right now."

"Is there anyone who could stay with you while your mother is in the hospital? I don't think you ought to be here alone. It wouldn't help your mother's recovery if she were worried about you."

"I don't think she cares much what happens to me," Karen said tersely.

"That's not true, Karen, and you know it. She's very concerned about you," Dr. Smyzer said in a reproving voice. "Right now, however, things are so distorted for her she can't react normally. But don't ever make the mistake of thinking she doesn't care about you."

Karen felt ashamed.

"Could you stay at a friend's house for a week or so?"

Karen thought of Jennie. She knew the Simmonses would welcome her, but she couldn't ask them to let her stay. If her mother had broken her leg or something, it would be different, but what kind of a name did you give this sickness?

"I can call my grandmother," she said.

"Good. How long will it take her to get here?"

"It's only a few hours on the train."

"Call her tonight. That hypodermic I gave your mother should keep her in good shape until tomorrow morning. I'll have a room ready for her by then. Can you arrange for your dad to drive her to the hospital?"

Karen hesitated. "I don't think I'd better ask him. It just upsets Mother to have him around."

"You're probably right," Dr. Smyzer said. "I'll tell you what. I'll drop by here and pick her up myself. Can you have her ready by eight in the morning?"

"I guess so," Karen said. "Do you think she'll give me any trouble about going to the hospital?"

"I think she'll be happy to have someone make the choices for her now. You just tell her I said she was to come along with no foolishness. Pack up her toothbrush and anything else she'll need."

When Dr. Smyzer left, Karen went back to the telephone. She sighed as she picked it up and dialed OPERATOR.

"Long distance?" Karen asked. "I'd like to place a person-to-person call to Mrs. Laura Newsome."

Karen gave the operator all the necessary information and waited for the call to go through. There was a momentary clicking sound after the ring, and then a brisk voice said,

"Laura Newsome speaking."

"Oh, Grandma," Karen said. "It's so good to talk to you."

"Karen? Is that you?"

"Yes, Grandma. We need you here. Can you come right away?"

3.

The Gray New Year

Having Grandmother Newsome around was like living with a hummingbird and a tornado all rolled into one. The Beal house seemed to vibrate on its foundations because of all the activity promoted by the slightly built but energetic woman. She never seemed to stop working for a moment. Even when she announced, "I think it is time for us to take a little rest," and settled in a rocking chair, her fingers continued to move rapidly as she mended, or embroidered, or knitted.

Karen was certain that her own room had never been cleaner. There were no more lazy mornings with nothing to do but sleep late. The first day Grandmother was there, Karen found herself unloading her closet and each of her dresser drawers, and examining each item of clothing carefully. Missing buttons were located and sewed on, zippers were checked and replaced if necessary. Old shoes were either polished or disposed of. Karen had to admit that all of this methodical cleaning had advantages.

There was also a wholesome regularity about meals, now that Grandmother was here. Karen hadn't realized how unappetizing the hastily assembled snacks of peanut butter or cheese sandwiches had been, when Mother wasn't able to prepare dinner. Now, Karen sat down hungrily to juicy slices of her grandmother's meat loaf served with baked potato and a crisp tossed salad, or a bowl of steaming stew bright with carrots and peas.

Most comforting of all, Karen felt that at last she had someone she could talk to about what was happening between her father and mother. Grandmother would be a formidable ally in bringing about a reconciliation.

Karen suggested this one evening while she was helping Grandmother with the dishes.

"Do you think there's anything we could do to convince Dad that he should come home?"

Karen thought for a moment that her grandmother was not going to answer. Her usually cheerful mouth straightened out into an unfamiliarly stern line. Then she said, "I hope when your mother gets out of the hospital, she will have the good sense to stop all this foolishness and do what she knows is right. Then your father will come home."

Karen was puzzled by the tone of Grandmother's answer. "Grandma, do you think this trouble is all Mother's fault?"

Grandmother paused thoughtfully with her hands still in the dishwater. "It's my fault in a way. I should have done more to help her learn what marriage is. When she was a young girl, she spent a lot of time reading books. She filled her head with a lot of silly ideas about romance. She never wanted to accept the fact that life wasn't all music and flowers and pretty dresses. She never was very good at making the best of unpleasant situations."

Karen picked up a wet plate and thoughtfully buffed it with the dish towel. Grandmother had always been a no-

nonsense type of person, but her explanation of the situation didn't satisfy Karen. The way Grandmother talked about marriage, it sounded like some sort of bad bargain that Mother had to endure. Karen thought of Mr. and Mrs. Simmons, and was sure they didn't feel that way. They seemed to enjoy being together.

Grandmother apparently had no use for romantic ideas about marriage, and she hadn't even mentioned the word "love." Karen had always thought of her grandmother as something of an authority on almost every subject. Now she began to wonder if Grandmother could be wrong.

Karen was just putting the last of the dried silverware into the drawer when the phone rang.

"Hi, Karen."

She recognized Jennie Simmons' voice.

"Hi. I was going to call you this evening," Karen said.

"How's your mother?" Jennie asked.

"Not much to report. The doctor says she needs complete rest." Karen hadn't really explained the entire problem to Jennie. There was always the unspoken factor of Dad's being away from home, but neither girl mentioned it. Undoubtedly, Gary had mentioned it to his family, and Jennie couldn't help knowing that something was wrong at the Beal house. It was unlikely that Jennie had failed to observe certain irregularities when she had visited Karen. Karen was grateful to Jennie for her tactful avoidance of the subject.

"What have you been doing?" Jennie asked lightly.

"Grandmother and I have been cleaning the house. You'd think she was getting us ready for an inspection by the general of the armies," Karen said in mock dismay.

"We've got something cooked up for New Year's Eve," Jennie said, in her usual bubbly voice.

Karen scooted a chair closer to the phone with the toe

of her brown loafer. She flopped down on it so she could listen more comfortably.

"What's the deal?"

"It's not really a party," Jennie said, "but we thought it might be fun to drive out to my uncle's farm tomorrow afternoon. Mom and Dad want to cut some more wood for the fireplace. There's a nice pond, and we could all go skating. We can't stay too late, because Gary has to start back to Northwood on New Year's Day, and Mom wants him to get to bed early."

Karen wondered if Gary ever saw Cliff up at school. Since Cliff was older, they probably didn't cross paths very often on campus.

"Who is going along?" Karen asked.

"Mom and Dad said each of us could invite one friend."

"Can you get so many people in your car?"

"Gary is asking Marty Riffner to go. Marty will probably take his car. We could go with him and let Mom and Dad take the little kids."

"Sounds great," Karen said. "Let me see what my grandmother says."

"I don't know, Karen," her grandmother said hesitantly. "I'm not sure I like the idea of you going on one of these New Year's Eve parties."

"It's not what you think," Karen protested. "Jennie Simmons is my best friend. Her parents and all her little brothers and sisters are going."

"I guess, since it's a family party, it will be all right."

Karen turned back to the phone. "All set, Jennie. Can I bring anything?"

There was a pause while Jennie talked to her mother, and then she said, "Mother says you can fix a plate of pickles and other relishes, if you wish. We'll pick you up about one o'clock tomorrow afternoon."

Karen spent the rest of that evening brushing and pressing her good brown slacks and washing and setting her hair. She went to bed with dreams of herself and Gary skating hand in hand on a picturesque pond.

THE NEW YEAR'S EVE party didn't turn out exactly as Karen had envisioned it in her imagination, and she was even more discouraged because she was aware that part of its failure was her own fault. Even though her better judgment warned her that this wasn't a date with Gary, she had hoped it would turn out that way. It didn't.

Much to Karen's disappointment, Marty and Gary sat in the front seat of the car with ten-year-old Joey, who had adamantly refused to ride in the Simmons' car with so many girls. Karen and Jennie found themselves crowded into the back seat of the old club coupe with Joey's friend, a large thermos of hot chocolate, and all the ice skates.

It was impossible to conduct any sort of intelligible conversation because the two small boys monopolized every second of silence. They giggled and laughed and talked at a pitch which rose higher and higher as each tried to be heard above the other. During most of the ride out to the farm, the ten-year-olds shouted riddles back and forth.

Joey's little buddy didn't ever seem to remember the proper ending to a riddle.

"Why did the little moron tiptoe across the medicine cabinet?" he shrieked, with the volume that only a ten-year-old boy can muster.

"Why?" Marty would shout back, almost as loudly.

"Because he____ah____he____ahhhh," the boy would stammer, vainly trying to think of the punch line. Karen

48

gritted her teeth and wondered why she had decided to come along.

"I know it. I've got it now," the boy would howl with delight at remembering. "The little moron didn't want to wake up the aspirins."

"Hey, you're marvelous," Marty said. "Wait'll I tell that one at school. I think you've started a whole new era of joke-telling. I'll call them goof-ball jokes."

Karen didn't know why everyone at school thought Marty was such a terrific guy. He was acting like an idiot. It made Karen doubly annoyed that Gary seemed to be enjoying the commotion every bit as much as Marty. Karen had given him credit for more intelligence than that. She shrugged herself angrily into the far corner of the back seat and kept her face turned toward the window. She complimented her own good judgment that she wasn't adding one word to the whole inane performance.

In Karen's estimation, things changed for the worse when they all arrived at the farm. Marty parked behind the Simmons' station wagon, and Karen watched in dismay as the twins and their friends spilled out of the car and darted about the yard like a swarm of bees in a field of buttercups.

Karen was aware that she and Marty were being introduced to the Simmons' aunt and uncle, but with all the confusion, it was impossible to do more than nod an acknowledgment.

When the turmoil became almost unbearable, Mr. Simmons grabbed Joey and his pal by the shoulders and held them firmly.

"Now, hear this," he commanded, and miraculously all the little Simmonses quieted down long enough for him to say, "Uncle Chris and I will take care of the wood-cutting.

You big kids handle the little sprouts. I don't want them fooling around close to the chain saw."

"Gary, you and Marty check the ice on the lake carefully," instructed Mrs. Simmons. "You set the boundaries and see that they skate where it's safe."

Karen thought disagreeably that she didn't care much if the whole gang fell in. It might give them some peace and quiet.

Karen felt a small mittened hand thrust into hers, and soon she was being dragged toward the pond. There she found herself involved in the business of unknotting and tying the long laces on several pairs of shoe skates. Her dreams of skating off alone with Gary were as cold as the brisk wind that had started to blow.

The six small children demanded constant attention as they cried out, "Watch me, Marty."

"Help me, Gary."

After a couple of hours spent in a monotonous routine of skating round and round the pond with a twin gripping each of her hands, Karen asked hopefully, "Aren't you two getting awfully cold? Your lips look blue to me."

The little girls nodded.

Karen suggested, "Why don't you and your little girl friends all run back to the house and drink some of that good hot chocolate your mom brought along in thermos jugs?"

"That's a good idea," Rosemary said. "Can you help us get our skates off?"

"Gladly," Karen said with relief. "Skate over and sit on that old log."

Karen knelt and slipped off her furry mittens, so she could get at their long shoe laces.

Gary skated up near them, and stopped with a shower of ice.

"Are you kids giving up?" he asked.

"They're very cold," Karen said quickly. "I suggested they go to the house for some hot chocolate."

She motioned toward Joey and his friend. "Might be a good idea for all the kids to do that. We've been out here for over two hours. We wouldn't want them to catch cold."

"I don't want to go back," Joey objected. "Let the girls go if they can't take it, but I'm not cold."

Gary looked at him. "You're not kidding anyone. You're cold all right."

"Come on, Gary," his younger brother pleaded. "Don't spoil the fun."

"I'll tell you what. We'll compromise," Gary said good-naturedly. "You boys help me gather some of the brush around the pond. Get some old dried branches, too. We'll build a bonfire."

The little girls had started toward the house, but turned back when they heard Gary's idea.

"Why don't we bring the thermos of chocolate out here? Then everyone can have some and warm up by the fire," Rebecca said.

"Good idea," Gary called to them. "You girls bring some of Aunt Carrie's kitchen matches back with you."

Before long they were all standing around the crackling fire drinking mugs of chocolate. Karen shifted positions as the wind altered and blew smoke in her eyes. As she moved around and stood near Marty, he leaned toward her and whispered, "Well, Moody Matilda. What's chewing on your woodwork today?"

Karen glared at him. "Not that it's any of your business,

but I didn't know I was going to have to spend the entire day baby-sitting."

"Why don't you just make the best of the situation?" Marty said. "You might have some fun in spite of yourself."

Karen turned toward him quickly. "What made you say a thing like that?"

Marty held up his hands in mock horror. "Look, let's not get psycho about it. I was trying to give you a clue on how to improve your love life."

Karen stepped back just as Joey and his friend began another bout of their constant wrestling. Joey slammed into Karen, spilling the cupful of hot chocolate she held. It splashed ugly fingerlets of brown liquid on the front of her pale tan car coat.

"Oh, no," she groaned. "That's all I needed."

The two little boys stopped their frolic and looked at her.

"Gee, we're sorry, Karen," Joey said. "We didn't mean to do it."

"Come on," Jennie said. "Let's go back to the house and get it cleaned off before it stains permanently."

"I'd really rather go by myself," Karen snapped.

Karen grabbed her skates by their long laces and ran, half-stumbling, through the frozen stubble of the field toward the farmhouse.

The wood-cutting and loading were all finished. The adults were inside, sitting in front of the big brick fireplace in the living room, drinking hot spiced tea and talking.

"Why, Karen," Mrs. Simmons exclaimed, when she saw Karen's soiled coat. "What happened?"

"There was an accident with the chocolate," Karen said, taking a grim satisfaction in not revealing Joey as the culprit.

"I think I can fix this up," Aunt Carrie said, and took Karen's coat from her and disappeared into the kitchen.

"Come here by the fire and get warm," Mrs. Simmons invited.

Karen sank down on a frayed old chair near the blaze. Idly she thumbed through some ancient copies of *Life* magazine. She'd seen most of them before, but she had to do something to keep from thinking about what had just happened out by the pond. In addition to that, Karen was disturbed by what Marty had said to her. She didn't like to be accused of being a poor sport. Did he think she enjoyed feeling the way she did? It affected everything that happened. It seemed as though nothing went right for Karen any longer.

As she sat staring at the old magazines, the crackling fire made her warmer and drowsier. The next thing Karen was aware of was a hand on her shoulder, shaking her gently. It was Jennie.

"Hey, sleepyhead. Wake up," Jennie called. "It's time to eat."

Karen sat up, embarrassed that she had dozed off. She joined the others at the table and sat numbly silent through the noise of dinner.

Early in the evening they loaded up the cars and were on their way home again. If she had hoped for any occasion to be alone with Gary, she had hoped in vain. There seemed to be no evidence that he was slightly interested in being alone with her. Why should he be? She hadn't proved herself much fun to be with.

When the others got out of the car, Marty asked, "Want to come up here in the front seat?"

"No thanks," Karen replied obstinately. "I'm fine back here."

Marty started the car with a jerk and drove her home.

As Karen got out of the car, Marty said, "I'll see you at school. I hope you're feeling better by then."

"I'm feeling just fine," Karen said.

"Okay, okay! You just seemed sort of lemonish all day."

"Does everything have to be rah-rah-rah all the time?" Karen asked curtly.

"No, but I thought you weren't having much fun."

"I didn't know anyone cared," she said.

"Skip it," Marty answered, and Karen knew he was angry. "I wanted to make sure you were happy so you don't goof on the next edition of the paper."

"I'll make sure my page of the *Crier* is ready on time and good enough to suit even your excellent standards, Horace Greeley."

Karen got out of the car and slammed the door. What a way to end an evening—New Year's Eve at that! What difference did it make anyway? Things weren't going to be magically transformed at the stroke of twelve. She'd wake up tomorrow and the same old problems would still be there.

4.

Break with the Past

Life for Karen leveled out to a daily routine of school, homework, and helping her grandmother around the house.

After spending two weeks in the hospital, Mother came home briefly to pack her bags. Then she left for a neighboring state to establish legal residence, so that she could obtain a divorce quickly and quietly.

Karen heard her mother and grandmother talking behind the closed bedroom door the day before Mother left. Karen knew it was wrong to listen, but she really couldn't help herself.

She could hear her grandmother saying, "You know it's wrong, Edna. You'll have to admit that."

Her mother replied in an unsteady voice, "It's not any more wrong than the marriage was in the first place. Now all I have left is the choice between two wrongs. I've decided to pick the lesser of two evils."

"You'll have to live with this decision the rest of your life," Grandmother continued. "You may regret it bitterly."

Karen pressed closer to the door to hear her mother's reply.

"It wouldn't be the first decision I've lived with and regretted. Why do you think I've been in the hospital for the last two weeks? Why do you think I've been nearly driven out of my mind for the past several months?"

There was a long silence. Karen started to move away from the door, thinking they were coming out into the living room. Then she heard her grandmother again.

"You've been ill because your mind tells you that what you're doing is wrong—disgraceful. You're not going to find any happiness this way."

That was all there was to the conversation. Karen couldn't really understand her grandmother's attitude, but then she didn't really understand anyone's attitude about the whole situation.

She wrote to Cliff, hoping that he might come home and find some way to stop the divorce. When he answered, he told her abruptly that she was too young to understand all the implications of the situation, and it was really none of her business.

None of her business? Did Cliff think she lived in a vacuum? Perhaps he could pretend it shouldn't affect their lives, since he was away at school now.

Her worry seemed to infect her schoolwork, too. No matter how long Karen sat working over her books, she couldn't really concentrate on Spanish or history, or even on the page she edited for the *Crier*.

"You're about ten inches short of copy again this week," Marty said accusingly.

"I can't be," Karen protested. "Look, here's the dummy sheet right here."

Marty took the make-up sheet out of her hand and looked it over, making pencil checks on it as he went through a sheaf of typewritten articles in his hand. He stopped and waved the papers at her.

"You put plenty of stories on the dummy, but you haven't turned them in. Somebody has missed a deadline. I can't read your scribbles. Who is it?"

Finally she said, "I guess it's my fault, Marty. I forgot to assign this story to anyone. What's in the filler box? Can't we use one of those?"

"Listen, Karen. This has happened three weeks in a row."

"I'm sorry, Marty," she said heatedly. "I said it was my fault, but I don't see what else we can do now. It's too late to assign a new story."

"You might sit down and write something yourself," he snapped at her.

Karen shook her head. "Marty, I can't. I'm sorry but I . . ." she couldn't tell him that her creativity seemed to have evaporated lately.

She flinched as he said, "I'll do it myself, then. We aren't even going to get a dishonorable mention at this rate. The next time you plan to foul out, let me know a little sooner. I don't want to wind up writing your whole page one of these days."

Karen was so angry she was tongue-tied. All he thought about was his precious state journalism rating. Didn't he understand that sometimes people had so many problems they couldn't think straight?

Karen walked unhappily through the hallways of the school to keep from crying. She heard the last bell ring, and she hurried from the building.

As the hurt and anger within her began to subside, she slowed down and realized that she had walked almost all the way uptown. She wasn't more than three blocks from her dad's office. It occurred to her that she hadn't seen him in quite a while.

Dad was talking on the telephone when she came into the small office. He motioned to her to sit down, but the office chairs were all piled high with old newspapers and magazines, colorful brochures, and typewritten sheets.

"Yes, yes," he said, rubbing his forehead and eyes as he talked. "I do have the abstract of the Jenson property. It's here in the office. I can check on that matter for you now if you'll hold the line a minute while I get the papers."

He placed the phone on his cluttered desk. The receiver slid off and dangled forlornly by its cord. He ignored it and began digging through the scrambled heap of documents.

"Can I help?" Karen asked.

He nodded and said, "I'm looking for a manila folder with legal-size paper, thick—about twenty-five pages. There's a typed sticker on the outside that says, 'Jenson Tract, 62A.' "

Karen could hear sputtering sounds coming from the earpiece of the phone. Dad picked it up.

"I've got it right here. Please, can't you hang on for a minute?" He paused. "Yes, I understand that you're a busy man, but so am I. I know it's here and I'd like to get it settled right now."

Karen made a muffled sound of triumph as she located the missing document and handed it to Dad.

"It's right here," he said, and Karen detected a relieved tone in his harried manner. "I'm trying to find the right section. Hold on, please."

Karen didn't like the pleading sound of her dad's conversation. She noticed that his hands were shaking as he thumbed through the pages of the abstract.

Karen turned away so that she didn't have to watch him in his obvious discomfort. She busied herself sorting out the hodgepodge on the chairs and desk. She had separated several magazines, newspapers, and brochures into neat piles and had begun alphabetizing manila folders when the phone conversation ended.

Dad sank down on the swivel chair behind the desk which Karen had just cleared off. His face was the sallow color of the papers he held in his hands. He rubbed the bridge of his nose with his fingers in a weary gesture.

Dad sighed and said, "That fellow has been camped on my doorstep for weeks. He thinks all I have to do is run a personal counseling service for his pleasure."

"Look, Dad," Karen offered eagerly. "I've got a great idea. I could come down to the office after school every day and help out. I could type letters for you and answer the phone and do your filing.

"I could help you clean up this mess, Dad," she said. "I don't know how you can do any work in all this jumble of papers. It's just too much for you to handle alone."

Dad stood up abruptly, pushing the swivel chair back so hard it crashed into the wall behind him. He turned and went into the small room at the back of the office. Karen stepped to the doorway and watched him mix a bicarbonate of soda. He swallowed the foaming liquid quickly, and then rinsed out the glass.

"Dad, I'm sorry if I said something wrong. I didn't mean to upset you. . . ."

She looked around the room where her dad had been staying for the past several weeks. It was as disorganized as the front office. There was a folding cot with a sleeping bag crumpled up on it. There was an open suitcase on a folding wooden chair. The table top was covered with miscellaneous items ranging from his razor and toothbrush to three cans of cream of chicken soup, a can opener, and an old hot plate. Karen shuddered inwardly. It seemed degrading for him to live like this.

"It's all right, Karen," he said, shaking his head as though he were trying to clear cobwebs out of his line of vision. "I'm sure you meant well, but . . ." he paused and shrugged. "It doesn't help me to be reminded that I can't handle my own business. I know things are far from what they ought to be. Goodness knows, your mother told me often enough how incompetent I am. She jammed that information down my throat every day of the world. There's just so much criticism a man can take. I didn't choose this business, she did!"

Karen felt frightened. His outbursts always left her shaky. She didn't know what to do.

"I'd better head home," she said. "Grandmother will wonder where I am."

He caught her arm and pulled her back. "Wait a minute. I'm sorry. I shouldn't blame you. It isn't your fault."

Karen thought sullenly that it seemed to be the first time she hadn't been at fault for a long time.

"Sit down, Karen," he said, pulling her toward a chair.

"I've been on edge lately." Then he laughed grimly. "Lately? That's a mild understatement. I've been on edge for years, but that's going to change. As soon as the divorce comes through and I find out where I stand financially, I'm going to chuck this whole business. It's going to be like getting out of prison."

Karen couldn't believe what she was hearing.

"Dad, I thought . . ." Karen tried to find just the right words to express her confusion. "I thought you loved this business."

She wasn't sure whether it was wise to continue, but she gathered courage to finish the sentence. "You spend more time here than you do at home."

"That's just the point," he said, and Karen was appalled at the bitterness in his voice. "I couldn't get away from it for a minute. It wasn't *my* business. I didn't own it—it owned me."

Karen had difficulty reconciling this outburst of Dad's with the picture she had built through the years—that this office was Dad's other love, and that Mother had helped him get something he had wanted.

"At first, I didn't know it was going to be like this. I had to do something when I got out of the army. I didn't have much training for anything except the farm work I'd done as a boy. Your mother thought this business would be a good deal, so I went along with her. I always gave in to your mother too easily."

Karen watched him move restlessly about the office as he talked.

"Your mother dazzled me when I met her. She was very pretty, and she laughed a lot, and I had a good time when I was with her. She wasn't like any other girl I had ever met. I suppose we really didn't know each other very well when we were married, but with a war on there wasn't time. I still remember being amazed that she agreed to marry me."

He stopped for a moment, and ran his fingers through his thinning hair. "She was always so much better at expressing herself than I was. I let her convince me that running this business was the right job for me. Gradually, she began to change, or maybe I got to know her better. She has a great deal of ambition. She likes expensive things. She drives people. She tried to make me into something I could

61

never become. She hates me because I failed. And I . . ." he broke off the sentence in the middle.

In a way, Karen was glad he didn't finish it, because she had an idea of what he had been about to say. It seemed so fantastic to be sitting here watching her dad painfully recalling the past. It was almost inconceivable to her to think that Mother and Dad could hate each other.

Karen didn't know what to do at that moment. There didn't seem to be anything for either Dad or her to say. She was going to ask if there wasn't any way to stop the divorce, to plead that he and Mother sit down and try to settle their differences reasonably. She knew now there was no use. Everything seemed to be at a dead end. She didn't even want to think about what tomorrow would be like.

She was grateful when the phone on the newly cleared desk began to ring. It gave her an excuse to break off this most unsatisfactory conversation.

"I'd better get home, Dad," she said. "Grandmother will wonder where I've been all this time."

He didn't try to detain her. Instead he turned his attention to the phone call.

As Karen left the office and went to the bus stop, she knew her grandmother would scold her for getting home so late and causing her to worry; but somehow it didn't really seem important.

WHEN Edna Beal returned home, the divorce was an accomplished fact. Karen looked at her mother curiously to see if some phenomenon had occurred to make her appear outwardly different, now that she was no longer married to Glen Beal.

At least Mother didn't have those terrible headaches which had kept her lying in a darkened room with a cold cloth over her eyes. She seemed to have recovered the intense energy which had animated her in the past, but Karen sensed that her mother wasn't quite the same as she had been. There was no joy in the frantic way she moved about doing the things which had to be done. There was no laughter in the large dark eyes with the lacy lashes—eyes that had once seemed like deep wells, overflowing with sparkling merriment. Her eyes now seemed dull and masked, as though shutting out any attempt to know what she was really thinking or feeling.

Edna Beal returned home on the morning of March ninth. By the eleventh of that month, she obtained employment as a switchboard operator in the business office of the *Evening Dispatch.* She rented a small apartment right downtown, just a few blocks from the building where the *Dispatch* presses were.

Karen hated the third-floor apartment with a sickening intensity. Her mother pointed out that it was clean, convenient, and not too expensive. Karen saw only that it was across town from Linden Street, and it was much smaller than the house they were now living in. The three rooms included a tiny living room, an efficiency kitchen with a small nook for the table, and a crowded bedroom furnished with twin beds which she and her mother would share.

As the process of moving became a reality, Karen discovered to her dismay that there was little room in the new apartment for many of their belongings.

Cliff came down from Northwood for a few days to help with the moving. He rented a truck and insisted on doing most of the actual physical part of the task. He carried boxes out to the truck, unloaded things at the apartment, and then returned to the house for more. In spite of the numerous things that had been discarded, Karen was amazed at how many trips it took to make the transfer from house to apartment.

Throughout the entire process, Cliff remained silent and uncommunicative. When Mother went into his room to supervise packing, he said, "I'll take care of this. Most of my stuff is up at school. I'll give the rest of this away, or throw it away. I don't want it any more."

Cliff insisted on packing up Dad's belongings, too. Mother didn't argue, but rather seemed relieved to let him take care of it and thereby avoid a face-to-face confrontation with Dad.

During the ordeal of moving, the situation was made even more disagreeable for Karen by the constant interruptions of people coming to the door to answer the newspaper advertisement Mother had placed. They invaded the old frame house, poked around in closets, and examined furniture, asking prices and making comments about the condition of the objects Mother had offered for sale. It made Karen angry to see their things examined and criticized by strangers.

She went into the back room where Cliff was packing.

"It's like attending your own funeral," she muttered.

"I guess you'll manage to live through it," he said, unsympathetically.

That was the way it was. Cliff rejected every attempt Karen made to talk to him about what had happened. She would have given anything to know what he was feeling. It would have helped if they could share this change in their lives together, have commiserated with each other, but the old bantering closeness they had once had seemed to be gone. Cliff was businesslike about the whole procedure. She couldn't analyze his attitude.

It seemed as though everyone in the family had been changed somehow by the divorce. Grandmother was stern and disapproving. Mother was moving mechanically through life. Dad was like a man searching for an escape hatch. Cliff had the most indefinable quality of all. He was so remote and withdrawn. And Karen wondered vaguely what sort of metamorphosis had occurred in her character. She couldn't describe it or label it. She knew its symptoms. She cried easily and was hurt easily. She felt as though her entire being was a raw sore which had become extremely sensitive to contact with others and caused her intense pain.

So the moving process continued like the transplanting of a young bit of delicate vegetation. It was removed from its familiar and comfortable surroundings. Just enough of the old habitation was retained to keep the roots from withering away.

Karen objected strenuously to the location of the apartment. "It's in another school district, Mother. What am I going to do?"

"You'll transfer to Central High. It's only a few blocks from the apartment," her mother said in a businesslike tone.

"Go to another school?" Karen asked, speaking louder than she had intended. "I can't do that."

Her mother had looked at her disapprovingly. Karen could not detect any sympathy or understanding in the reply.

"Of course you'll transfer. Other students have done it."

"But all my friends are at Marshall."

"You'll make new friends. Teen-agers are the same everywhere. You'll soon find that out."

"You don't understand, Mother," Karen tried again, frustrated that she couldn't seem to break through her mother's shell of resistance. "I've been in all sorts of activities at Marshall. There's the Speech Club and Girls' Athletics. It's practically a cinch that I'll be elected editor of the *Town Crier* for next year. I want to graduate from Marshall with Jennie and the rest of the kids."

"Karen, I know that it seems hard to think about making a change, but you'll have to make up your mind to adjust."

Karen's face was flushed with anger. "I'll lose all my service credits. They won't mean a thing at another school. I have a chance for honors at graduation. If we move, it will all go down the drain."

"If you did well at one school, you'll do well at another," her mother said, with a calm reasonableness that infuriated Karen.

"It just doesn't work that way. . . ."

Her mother stopped packing for a moment. The lines around her eyes hardened. "Lower your voice this instant, and stop being foolish. I will not continue the argument. We have to move, Karen. There is no other alternative. I will not be earning enough to manage a house this size. It's too large for just the two of us, anyway. We no longer have a car; that went to your father. I'll have to live close enough to work so that I can walk."

"Doesn't the court make Dad pay part of our expenses?" Karen asked. "What about alimony?"

"Where did you get ideas like that?" her mother demanded. "To whom were you talking about alimony?"

"I haven't been talking to anyone, but I've read articles in magazines about this sort of thing. I'm not completely in the dark," Karen hesitated, and then recklessly added, "even though you've tried your best to keep me that way."

"Don't be rude to me, young lady!"

"But doesn't he?" Karen insisted. "Doesn't Dad have to pay something?"

"He is required to pay a small amount called child care, but it won't begin to cover your expenses," her mother said. "There is no alimony. I did not ask him for a cent. I didn't want anything from him but our freedom."

Our freedom! Did Mother think a whole family divorced each other? *Perhaps they do,* Karen conceded bitterly. They would all be living in different places. Karen would visit her dad during vacations. Cliff seemed to be resigned to existing in a kind of limbo. When he wasn't at college, he'd really have no place that was home. He'd be a visitor everywhere—at the apartment and at Dad's place. There'd be two houses but no home.

Freedom? Karen didn't see this as freedom. She was being forced to accept a situation she didn't like at all. No one had asked her if she wanted to be a part of the divorce. She was a member of the family, but she had no voice in the decision to dissolve it. She hadn't wanted to split up. She didn't want to leave Marshall High and the activities she enjoyed there. She didn't want to move away from her friends.

Almost before Karen knew what she was doing, she had slammed down the pile of old magazines she held in her arms. They hurtled to the floor with a loud thud and skidded about on their slick covers.

"It's not fair," she shouted at her mother. "Why do I suffer for something I didn't even want to happen in the first place? I won't move and you can't make me."

Karen ran to her room and got her coat. She started back through the house to the front door.

Her mother followed her and grabbed her arm but Karen twisted away.

"You're just like your father," her mother said to her.

No one had to draw a diagram for Karen to know that

the comparison with her dad was not intended as a compliment.

"You rage and shout and storm around." Her mother's words were like darts aimed at her. "You blame me for everything that displeases you."

Karen pulled on her coat and opened the door, but her mother blocked her exit.

"Run off when the going gets rough," her mother flung at her. "Everyone else can walk out, but I have to stay and pick up the pieces. It's always been up to me to keep this family on its feet. Somebody around here had to have some backbone. And if you think the last twenty years have been a picnic for me—if you think I've been able to do any of the things I've wanted to do, then you're sadly mistaken."

Her mother stepped away from the door, pale and shaken.

Outside the house, Karen pulled the coat collar up around her ears. She wished she had remembered to get a scarf to protect herself from the March winds that howled and complained in her ears. It reminded her of Mother's accusing voice.

Karen had no particular destination in mind when she left the house, but she walked instinctively toward Jennie Simmons' home. It would be warm and pleasant there.

The rest of the afternoon passed quickly. It was a little after six o'clock when Karen made herself leave the Simmons' place. She walked slowly back toward the frame house on Linden Street where Mother waited. Mrs. Simmons had asked Karen to stay and eat dinner with them. Karen would have liked that, but she couldn't help feeling a disturbing twinge of conscience about the way she had slammed out of the house, leaving Mother alone.

Karen also felt a bit of trepidation about the kind of reception she would get when she arrived back at the house. She was never quite sure of herself in a situation like this. Karen felt that she had been treated unfairly; and she was bewildered that, in spite of this, she should feel so guilty about arguing with her mother.

The lights were on in the kitchen, so Karen avoided the back door and went in through the front. She stood uncertainly in the darkened living room. She didn't know what to say to her mother, but she had made up her mind that she wouldn't apologize.

Summoning her courage, she went quietly into the kitchen where Mother was standing at the stove. Mother didn't turn around when Karen came into the room.

"Hang up your coat," her mother said in a restrained voice, "and then get a couple of bowls. I've made some chowder for us. Or did you eat dinner when you were over at Jennie's?"

"How did you know I was there?" Karen asked in surprise.

Her mother turned and faced her. She said in very controlled, yet pointed tones, "I know you very well, Karen, and I understand you better than you think I do."

After they had eaten the rich, creamy soup with potato and golden flecks of corn floating in it, Karen said, experimentally, "Mother, I know that we can't stay here in this house, but . . ."

Karen waited uncertainly for a moment, tested her mother's receptiveness to resuming the discussion. She sought the most tactful words. "Jennie said, . . . I mean, it was really Mrs. Simmons who suggested it. . . ." Karen couldn't look up at her mother's face, so she ducked her head and plunged into the subject rapidly. "What I'm trying to say is . . . the Simmonses have an extra room at their house because Gary is away at college, and . . ." Karen's thoughts raced ahead, and she had difficulty disciplining her voice as she hurried to say everything before her mother interrupted. "Anyway, they've asked me to come and stay with them so that I can finish school at Marshall."

Her mother didn't speak but got up from the table and began to clear away the supper dishes.

When her mother did speak, her voice shook with emotion, and Karen knew there was a deep reservoir of anger beneath the words.

"You had no right to discuss our private family matters with outsiders."

Karen was incredulous at such a statement. Her own voice quavered as she defended herself.

"Mother, they know that you and Dad are divorced. You can't keep a thing like that secret."

"And that is another very good reason why we are leaving this house and this neighborhood. I would leave this town if I could manage it. I would go where curious people do not know about us and gossip about things which do not concern them."

"But Jennie is my friend. The Simmonses are my friends. They wouldn't gossip about us. Besides, they offered to let me live in their home. Now why would they do that if they didn't want to help us?"

"Pity," her mother said grimly. "You must have told them quite a tale of woe. They're probably feeling very self-righteous to have made such an offer. They feel sorry for you because . . ." Mother's voice stayed on a high pitch, which indicated that there was more to the sentence that she couldn't bring herself to say out loud.

Karen finished the thought mentally, even though she didn't want to. *They feel sorry for you because . . . because you come from a broken home. Because all of this makes you different from other people, not quite as normal as they are.* Something inside Karen rebelled at this interpretation. That hadn't been the way the Simmonses had acted toward her. They didn't pity her . . . or did they? Why did things have to get so mixed-up?

Numbly, Karen dried the dishes, and then went to her room and lay across the bed in the darkness. She didn't cry. She seemed to have no tears left. She had to find a way out of the maze she was trapped in, but a solution didn't seem likely. She hadn't been able to solve any of the other problems the family had.

Karen heard the door creak slightly and she saw a narrow beam of light fall across the bed. Her mother was standing in the doorway.

"Karen," she called softly. "I've been thinking. There may be a way we can work this out. Don't get your heart set on it, because I haven't checked, and I don't know for certain whether we can work it out. I'll see about it tomorrow."

Karen sat up and waited eagerly.

"Perhaps we can get permission for you to attend Marshall even though we'll be living in another district. It won't be easy for you," her mother hastened to add. "You'll have to ride the city bus quite a distance."

"I can use the time on the bus to study," Karen said enthusiastically.

"If you can't keep your grades up, you'll have to transfer to Central after all."

"I can do it, I know I can," Karen promised excitedly. She stood up and hurried to her mother. She threw her arms about her and hugged her. She felt Mother's arms slowly encircling her. Karen realized how long it had been since either of them had expressed any affection for the other. Karen closed her eyes and put her head on her mother's shoulder. The two of them stood quietly.

"Mother, I didn't mean to hurt you by the things I said," Karen whispered in a choked voice.

She felt Mother's hand smoothing back her hair. "Karen, I love you very much. I know it may be hard for you to realize that, considering what has happened to us lately. This isn't the way I wanted things to turn out for all of us, but life has been so . . ." She paused, and Karen knew it was hard for Mother to speak. "Karen, dear, I just wish you could understand."

"I'm trying, Mother. I don't seem to know what is right or wrong anymore."

"You're not the only one who has that problem," Mother said, sighing with breath that seemed to come from her feet and move painfully through her whole body. "Karen, if there had been any other solution than . . . than divorce, I would have taken it gladly. I tried as long as I could to hold out against it. I lived for months, even years, beyond what I thought was the breaking point. I know divorce is wrong. I suffer the consequences of that knowledge every day I live, but the situation was so impossible. . . ." Another painful hesitation followed. "I just couldn't endure it any longer. There seemed to be no other way out. I honestly believed that the atmosphere in this house wasn't doing any of us any good. It would be better to end it."

Karen did not move away from her mother. There was consolation in holding each other close. There were so many questions Karen wanted to ask, so many things she wanted to say. Finally she found the voice to ask, "Mother, how can two people get married, and then stop loving each other? What happened?"

Karen felt Mother's arm drop from her. Mother took her hand and led her to the bed where they sat together with just the faint glow from the other room for light.

"Karen, I was twenty-two years old when I met your father. I married him a few months later. Things hadn't been easy for my family. Your Grandfather Newsome died when I was only eleven years old. Grandmother had to raise a very large family by herself. It was during the depression, and she supported us by working long, hard hours as a dressmaker. My brothers and sisters grew up and got married, leaving me home alone. Even my younger brother was married before I was. I was looking for someone very special, someone I could respect, someone I could love deeply.

"Your uncle and his bride shared a house with your grandmother and me. When the United States entered World War II, your uncle joined. One weekend, he brought an army buddy home. The buddy seemed to like me, and that pleased the family. He was nice enough, but . . ." Mother's words trailed off into nothingness.

At last, she said, "I dated him because there was nothing else to do. He made it clear to the family that he wanted to marry me. Your grandmother and uncle told me to use my head and get married. They said it would mean security for me. As I look back on it now, I think they felt that they would be relieved of the responsibility of taking care of me if I would get married and leave home. Their arguments began to make sense. I wanted a home and children, so I agreed to marry Glen Beal. When he came home after the war, I realized we didn't really know each other very well. I don't think he even knew himself. At least, he didn't know what he wanted to do. He finally got a job working in a filling station, but he wasn't happy there. Then he worked as a salesman in a shoe store. Later he was a fry-cook in an all-night restaurant. He changed jobs frequently. He never did have very good control of his temper. Sometimes he would get angry and simply walk away from a job and refuse to go back. I guess that is when I first began to have such terrible headaches. I worried constantly, because by this time we had a family to take care of.

"I thought it might make a difference if your dad had a business of his own. I went to work to get the money to set him up with his real estate office. I hated to leave you and Cliff with baby-sitters, but what else could I do? When we bought the business, I found I still couldn't stay home and be a full-time mother. I had to help out at the office. It wasn't easy to build up the business. There were times when your dad would become disgusted with a client. He'd lose his temper and a sale of property would be in jeopardy. I don't know how many hours I've spent trying to soothe the ruffled feelings of a client. Your dad seemed to resent my help more and more. He would get so angry that he'd walk out and leave me to run the business by myself.

"There never seemed to be enough money for the things we needed. We bought this old house, hoping to remodel it someday. We were lucky to be able to afford a coat of paint occasionally. It just got to be too much for me, Karen. I couldn't endure it."

They sat together, mother and daughter. Karen heard what Mother had to say. She remembered her talk with Dad in his office. She knew how Grandmother Newsome felt about the divorce. Somewhere there had to be that focal point of facts called truth, but right now Karen couldn't find it. It was like trying to form a picture using the pieces of several different jigsaw puzzles. Nothing matched.

5.

The Invitation

THE BUS ride across town seemed especially long that day in April. The weather was unseasonably warm, but Karen wore her jacket rather than carry it and add to the weight of the books she had brought home to study. Wearily she walked from where she got off the bus to the apartment building. Inside the lobby, she mechanically dialed the combination on the tiny metal door of their mailbox.

As she sorted the envelopes, half-heartedly, she discovered one addressed to her. It was postmarked Bluffton. In the return-address corner there was a blue and gold emblem of Northwood State College. At first she thought it might be a letter from her brother, Cliff. Just above the Northwood emblem, however, she noticed the tiny inked-in initials *G.J.S.*

Karen stared unbelievingly at the envelope for a moment. Then she grabbed up her books from the oblong table near the mailboxes where she had dumped them. She didn't even wait for the self-operating elevator to make its trip down to the main floor to pick her up. Instead, she dashed across the lobby and ran up the three flights of stairs to the apartment. Her hands fumbled with the key as she tried to get the door open. Papers spilled out of her notebook haphazardly, but she didn't care. She shoved the door open with her foot and tossed her books inside on the floor.

She glanced at the wall clock. She had fifteen minutes before Mother was due home. That would be fifteen minutes of complete privacy.

She flopped on the divan and very carefully slit the envelope open with her nail file. She wanted to preserve it intact. Hastily she read the contents.

> Dear Karen:
>
> I meant to write sooner, but I've been very busy during this second semester, and I didn't have your new address until just a few days ago, when Jennie sent it to me.

He had asked Jennie for her address! Jennie hadn't mentioned it to her, but maybe she was waiting to let Gary make the first move.

> I hope you're settled in your new place by now, and are happy in the apartment. Jennie says that you are still attending Marshall and take a city bus across town every day. I know that Jennie is glad you didn't transfer to another school. You two have been friends since I can remember.
>
> One reason I am writing is to ask if you can come up to Northwood for our Annual Invitation Weekend. The kids up here call it The Invite. There are several activities planned which I think you'll enjoy. The college orchestra is giving a concert Friday evening. On Saturday we can

visit classrooms, and then go to the all-college picnic. That night is the really big affair—The Invite Dance. It will be formal. On Sunday we attend the college chapel services together. You could take the train home in the afternoon. That would give you time to rest up or study Sunday night.

Arrangements are made for guests to stay in the dormitories. I thought you would like to stay with some of the girls here to get an idea of what college life is like. Who knows, you might decide that Northwood is the school you want to attend.

I'm trying to line up a date for Jennie, too, so that you girls can make the trip together.

Let me know as soon as possible if you can come so that I can sign up for a hostess and a room for you.

Please let me know what color dress you plan to wear to the dance.

Hoping to see you soon.

As ever,

Gary.

P.S. You may have a chance to visit with Cliff while you're here.

Karen lay back on the divan and closed her eyes. A whole weekend at Northwood near Gary. What fun to see him and be with him every day. She remembered how he had danced with her at his house on Christmas Day. She shivered with anticipation. She'd have to go about this very carefully, if she expected to persuade her mother to let her go to The Invite. *The Invite,* she repeated to herself. Crazy name, but how wonderful it was going to be. She wondered if she could possibly manage to get a new formal. She had three weeks to work on the problem.

Karen heard a noise outside the door. Quickly she looked at the clock. It couldn't be her mother yet. It must be another tenant out in the hallway, but Karen was spurred to action.

Quickly she stuck the letter from Gary into her Spanish book. She slipped off her jacket and hurried to the kitchen. She lit the gas burner under a pot of water to boil for spaghetti. She peeled and diced some onions, and was beginning to sauté them when she heard Mother come in.

"Hi," she called cheerily to her mother. "Are you starved?"

Her mother entered the brightly lighted kitchen. "Is there any mail?"

Karen thought of the letter from Gary which she had stuck inside her Spanish book. Better not mention it just now.

"Mostly advertisements," Karen said. "And a few bills, I think. I put your mail on the kitchen table. Why don't you relax for a while and look at it?"

Her mother gave her a grateful glance and sat down.

"Don't fix too much, " she said. "I'm really not very hungry."

Karen turned toward her mother. She was still terribly thin. Her face looked hollow and drawn. Karen wondered if she would ever regain her old sparkle.

Mother sorted through the uninteresting assortment of envelopes on the table. Karen had to restrain herself to keep from bubbling over with the news of Gary's invitation.

"Something funny happened at school today."

Her mother gave her something resembling attention, so Karen continued in her effort to enliven their conversation.

"We've got a sophomore girl on the staff who is a typist for the *Town Crier*. She's a nice kid, but kind of scatter-brained. She handed in a stack of copy she had typed up for next week's edition. She put it in the box marked 'print.'

"When Marty Riffner and I checked it over, we discovered that she had typed up her English grammar homework and mixed it in with the regular stories. Marty thought it would be hilarious if we printed it in the paper and gave her a by-line."

Karen noticed a faint smile flutter at the edges of her mother's mouth. She felt a compulsion to keep talking.

"Miss Gray thought Marty's suggestion was very funny, but didn't think it would help our news rating. Did you know that Miss Gray thinks we've got a good chance of winning a top award in the Class A division with the paper this year?"

Karen went to the refrigerator and got out some lettuce and tomatoes for a tossed salad.

"If I get to be editor next year, and IF we pull in another top rating, I'll have a good chance for the State Journalism Scholarship."

Her mother turned to her questioningly, "How are your grades, Karen?"

Karen hesitated. Perhaps she shouldn't have ventured into that area.

"I'm holding my own," she said.

Her mother sighed and stood up. "Just remember the bargain we made. You've got to get good grades or . . ."

"I know, Mother. Please don't worry."

Mother tossed the advertisements into the wastebasket. "I think I'll lie down until dinner is ready, if you don't mind."

"You don't have another one of those headaches, do you?"

Mother shook her head. "No, it's not that. I'm just tired. It's been a long day."

When dinner was ready, Karen went into the tiny bedroom to call her mother. She was asleep. The tense lines of her face had relaxed. Karen hated to disturb her now. She went back to the kitchen and prepared a tray with a salad, a vegetable, and a colorful plate of spaghetti. She carried it back to the bedroom.

"Mother," she called softly.

Mother's eyes opened slowly, and Karen said, "Here's your dinner in bed. Compliments of the house."

Her mother sat up and took the tray on her lap. Karen helped arrange pillows behind her back.

"After you eat, I'll do the dishes while you soak in a hot bath. Then you can go right to bed."

"Thank you, dear, but there are too many things that need to be done around the apartment. I've got to burn trash and do some laundry."

"I'll take care of the trash and the laundry. No problem."

"What about homework?" Mother asked.

"I'll take my books downstairs with me. I can study in the laundry room while I'm waiting for the clothes to wash and dry."

Mother seemed a bit uneasy. "Do you think you can really study that way?"

Karen laughed. "If I can study with my record player going, then I can surely study to the beat of the washer."

"This sudden enthusiasm for housework surprises me," Mother said in a joking tone. "I hope I'm not going to have to pay for it later."

Karen went back into the kitchen. She hadn't intended

her offer of help to turn out that way, but her mother had come closer to the truth than she knew.

While she ate at the kitchen table, Karen propped up her Spanish book so she could begin memorizing the new vocabulary list. The letter from Gary fell from between the pages. She couldn't resist opening it once more and reading it over quickly.

AFTER eating dinner and doing the dishes, Karen gathered up a load of clothes and put them in the large plastic laundry basket. On top she piled a box of soap powder, her notebook, and her Spanish and English texts. She was glad she had finished her geometry on the bus. She balanced the basket on one hip and held it with her left hand. She picked up the wastebasket and some matches in her right hand and headed toward the self-service elevator.

When she reached the basement, Karen walked through the dismal yellowish light of the hallway into the large laundry room. She set the controls of the washer, added soap, and then dumped in the clothes. She went to the far end of the room where the trash burner was. As she let the metal cover of the incinerator slide open, she noticed a box of papers on the floor by the burner. She looked at them more closely and discovered that the papers were covered with drawings. She stooped down and picked one up from the top of the pile.

It was a sketch done in pen and ink. She thought she had seen it before, but couldn't remember where. It depicted several men playing football with a distorted globe of the world.

Karen gathered up several other drawings from the box on the floor and looked through them. Some were rough sketches of persons. She recognized one of Babe Ruth.

Another was obviously Churchill, and a third was Charles de Gaulle. Some of the drawings were well executed and had the quality of portraits, while others were cartoons or caricatures.

As Karen stood looking at the pictures, she became aware of another person in the room with her. She whirled around, startled.

"I'm sorry if I frightened you," said a tall man standing behind her. "I suppose it was my ego that made me slip up on you unannounced. It's not often I see someone so engrossed in my work."

The man smiled broadly and Karen relaxed.

"Did you really draw these?" Karen asked, forgetting her embarrassment at having been discovered raiding someone's trash box.

He nodded and grinned again.

"They're wonderful," she said. "But what are they doing down here by the incinerator?"

"That's their final destination," he said.

"You aren't really going to burn them, are you?"

"I live in a very small apartment," he said. "It's either them or me."

Karen looked at him unbelievingly. "If I could draw like this, I wouldn't ever throw anything away."

"Young lady, you have made my day complete! Perhaps I'll make arrangements for you to come and talk to my boss. I'm sure he doesn't realize what a great talent I am. But, you see, all these drawings have served their purpose. They've been printed in the paper, and there's really no excuse to save them. I draw several sketches every day, so you can imagine how many I would have after twenty years at this work."

"I thought I had seen these somewhere before. Now I

know what they are," Karen said. "They're news cartoons from the editorial page of the *Evening Dispatch*."

"Now I am amazed. I didn't realize young people read anything but the comics."

"We do at school. Our journalism teacher makes us study the newspapers for layout and makeup. Wait until I tell her I've met you."

"I guess if you're going to be my publicity agent, I'd better tell you my name." He extended his hand to her. It was a large hand. Not the kind of hand Karen would have imagined an artist would have. "I'm Phillip Forrester," he said.

Karen smiled and shook his hand. "I'm glad to know you. I'm Karen Beal."

"You must be new in this apartment. I haven't seen you around before," he said.

"We've been here only a few weeks, and we're not around much of the time. My mother works. My brother, Cliff, is up at Northwood State College." She paused. There was an empty sensation in the pit of her stomach. It seemed strange not to mention Dad, but she didn't feel like making explanations. She continued, "I go to Marshall High."

He seemed surprised. "Marshall is on the other side of town, isn't it? Central is closer, and I understand they have a fine scholastic rating."

"I've heard that, but I don't want to leave all my friends and activities at Marshall."

"Did you say you're on the school paper?" he inquired, obviously interested.

"Yes. It's called the *Town Crier*. I edit the feature page." Karen glanced inadvertently at the drawings she still held. "Say, this gives me an idea. I think an article on how a news cartoonist works would make an interesting feature."

"I'd be very honored," he said.

"I can come to the *Dispatch* office any time you say it would be convenient for me to interview you. My mother works there, too."

"She does?" He seemed puzzled. "I don't think I know a Mrs. Beal. Is she new on the staff?" He added, rather apologetically, "Of course, I don't get down to the society department very often."

"Oh, she's not a reporter," Karen laughed. "She's a switchboard operator in the business office. She's only been there a short time."

"That is a coincidence. Why don't you come in after school tomorrow?" he suggested.

"I'll be there," Karen said. "And thank you very much."

Karen started back to the washing machine to check on the clothes, but turned toward Mr. Forrester, who was stuffing his drawings into the trash burner.

"Wait, Mr. Forrester," she called. "Do you mind if I take some of these?"

"Be my guest," he said. "Take all you want. They're free, and it does marvelous things for my self-esteem."

Karen smiled and picked up several of the drawings. She liked this big man with salt-and-pepper gray hair and a grin as wide as the Mississippi River.

6.

Something Gained

THE NEXT morning, Karen awoke to the tempting aroma of bacon coming from the kitchen. She dressed hurriedly and went into the kitchen, where Mother was setting the table.

"Breakfast is almost ready," she said. "I'll have hot cocoa ready for you in a minute. It's chilly outside. It's going to rain."

"Did you get a good night's rest?" Karen asked hopefully.

"Yes, I slept fairly well. I didn't even hear you come in last night. Did you get the washing all finished?"

Karen nodded, as she buttered toast.

"How about your homework?"

"Everything's ready. I'll be able to study my Spanish vocabulary again on the bus this morning, so I should be set for the test."

Karen knew she was making the situation sound much better than it actually was. She hadn't really been able to concentrate fully on her homework.

Mother sat down across from her and stirred sugar into a cup of hot coffee.

"Is coffee all you're going to have for breakfast?" Karen asked. "These eggs are good. Here, take one of mine." She shoved her plate toward Mother.

"No, thank you," Mother said, returning the dish. "I'm not very hungry."

Karen wished that Mother would have more than coffee to start the day. Karen thought her mother seemed far too gaunt since she had been in the hospital. On second thought, Karen decided to avoid any mention of a subject which might upset her mother.

Instead, she said, "I've got great plans for a feature story in next week's paper. I met a neighbor of ours while I was doing the laundry last night. He's an artist. He draws the news cartoons for the *Evening Dispatch*. Isn't that a co-incidence? You both work at the same place."

Karen flipped open her notebook on the kitchen table and spread his drawings out. Her mother looked through them casually.

"Isn't he talented?" Karen asked. "I want to run some of these sketches in the *Town Crier*. He's going to let me interview him about his work, so I'll be in the *Dispatch* building after school. We can walk home together when you get off work."

Karen cleared her breakfast dishes from the table. She wondered whether she should take this time to mention Gary's letter. Karen knew that she wouldn't be able to study at all today if she kept it to herself much longer.

"You'd better take your raincoat and boots, Karen," her mother reminded. "I don't want you to get soaked in a rainstorm."

Karen went into the other room to get her things. All the time her mind was busy wording and rewording sentences, trying to phrase the magic combination which would convince her mother that she should be allowed to attend The Invite.

"Mother," she began tentatively, as she tugged on the white fur-topped boots. "I've been invited to go up to Northwood to attend the annual invitational weekend. There will be a picnic, and a concert, and a dance. I think Jennie is going along, too. We'll stay in the women's dormitory."

"Have you heard from Cliff?" Mother asked unexpectedly. "Did he ask you to come up?"

"Oh, no," she said. "It wasn't Cliff. Gary Simmons invited me." Then she added quickly, "Gary said I will probably have a chance to visit with Cliff while I'm up there."

"Karen, I don't know what to say," her mother replied doubtfully.

"Don't make a decision yet," Karen begged. "It's almost time for me to catch my bus. Think it over today, and tell me when I see you tonight. But please remember, Mother, it's something the college planned. And it will be a good chance for me to see if I'm interested in attending Northwood."

Karen grabbed her books and plastic rain cap, and hurried out of the house toward the bus stop. As she ran, she reproached herself. She shouldn't have mentioned The Invite this morning. There hadn't been time to state her case effectively. But what other time was there to do it? Mother was always so tired when she came home from work at night that it wasn't a good idea to ask her then.

It was beginning to sprinkle when Karen got off the bus, half a block from school. Jennie was waiting for her, and the girls chattered excitedly about the prospects for going to Northwood.

"Keep your fingers crossed," Karen called after her at the school door.

Karen spent most of the morning staring at the identical round clocks high on the wall of each classroom. She listened for the small metallic click which announced the passing of one more minute in a long day. In English class she could not force herself to give complete attention to *The Tale of the Ancient Mariner*, even though she knew she was in danger of being caught unprepared by the questioning teacher. Spanish class wasn't much better. After she had handed in her test, she could not remember whether she had confused the Spanish words for "the trip" with "little old man." An interesting mistake if she should ever have an opportunity to use "viaje" or "viajo" in a conversation.

At noon, Karen met Jennie at the cafeteria.

"I'm going to pick up a sandwich and some pie," Karen said. "I want to eat in the journalism room. I've still got some work to do on the paper."

They carried their lunches into the large, cluttered room at the end of the hallway. Marty Riffner and several other staff members were also eating in the room on that rainy day.

Karen took a bite of the ham sandwich and a drink of milk from the paper carton. Then she started counting out headlines for stories on her feature page.

From the corner of the room came repeated guffaws of laughter. Karen kept losing count and having to go back and start over. It was almost impossible to think with all the racket going on.

"Hey, you kids," Karen said in an annoyed voice. "Keep it down to a loud roar, will you? I'm trying to do some work."

"If you'd pay attention in class instead of supervising

every tick of the clock, you wouldn't have to spend your lunch hour working," Marty said.

"He makes me so mad," Karen said to Jennie. "I wish he'd mind his own business."

Karen thought Jennie gave her a strange sidelong glance, but she didn't comment. Instead, Jennie continued to concentrate on her notebook and her American Government text.

"How can you think in this bedlam?" Karen inquired.

Jennie laughed. "I guess it all depends on what you're thinking about," she said, and shoved her notebook over so Karen could see it.

There were several pictures which had been cut out of fashion magazines. "These are ideas for my dress for The Invite dance. Mom is going to meet me after school, and we'll shop for material."

Karen looked at the pictures wistfully. It would be fun to have a new dress for the occasion. Gary had asked her to let him know what color she planned to wear.

"This is perfect for you," Karen said, indicating one of the pictures, and trying not to sound envious. Karen could visualize Jennie in the fluffy yellow dress. "It would emphasize your greenish eyes and dark hair."

"Listen," Jennie suggested, obviously sensing Karen's mood. "There's no reason why Mom and I can't help you make a dress, too. It's a lot cheaper than buying one ready made."

"I'd like to have something new," Karen agreed, "but I wouldn't want to spend money for a dress and then find out I'm not even going to get to go to The Invite."

"Is this the same girl talking who dared to buy ten dollars' worth of records before she even had a record player?"

"Things have changed a lot since Christmas."

Jennie touched Karen's arm gently. "I'm sorry. I didn't mean to be pushy. I know things are rough for you."

Karen pulled her arm away quickly. She didn't want any pity. "No need to get sticky about it," Karen said, more sharply than she intended. "I'll get along."

It was still raining intermittently when Karen got out of school and walked to the bus stop. She was glad she didn't have to wait long. She did want to look nice when she went to the newspaper office to interview Mr. Forrester.

K AREN went directly to the business office when she arrived at the *Dispatch* building. A stranger at the switchboard explained that Mrs. Beal was taking her coffee break. Helpfully, she offered to put Karen's books and rainwear under the counter until after the interview.

Upstairs, Karen walked cautiously into the large pressroom. She realized she didn't really know where to look for Mr. Forrester. She had visited the *Evening Dispatch* when she took Beginning Journalism, but that had been two years ago. She had been overwhelmed then by all the activity, and didn't really remember much about the building.

Karen looked around, and then walked toward a circular desk where wooden dividers separated the work areas. There were typewriters side by side in a continuous chain around the circumference of that desk.

Before it was necessary to disturb anyone, however, she saw a familiar face.

"Hello, Karen," Mr. Forrester said, moving toward her. There was a pencil stuck behind his ear. The top button of his shirt was unbuttoned, and he wore no tie. His sleeves were rolled up. In fact, he fitted the stereotype of a newspaperman exactly.

"I've been keeping an eye out for you," he said. "I was afraid you wouldn't be able to locate my little cubbyhole over there in the corner."

He broke a trail through the crowded room, and Karen followed him, dodging the people who moved about energetically. He pointed to a draftsman's table by the window. His area was glassed in on two sides, and gave the appearance of privacy.

"Good light here," he said. "It's out of the mainstream of traffic, but I can still see what's going on."

He scooted a chair closer to the table for her and indicated a box of sketches for her to look at.

"I've got a clearance sheet on any of these you might wish to reprint."

For the better part of the next hour, Karen made a vain attempt to make notes of all that Mr. Forrester told her. However, as he began to show her how he laid out his sketches and demonstrate the tools of his trade, it was impossible to jot down more than brief notes on his enthusiastic conversation.

"The main problem with a daily," he explained, "is trying to make a significant comment on the immediate political or national situation. Oh, it's fairly easy if there's a crisis. It's the relatively dry periods that are rough."

The more he talked, the more Karen realized how much he enjoyed his work and how well informed he was. She didn't think she had ever met a more interesting person.

"Anything else you care to know about?" he asked.

"I think you've covered it very well," she said. "After I write up the story, I'll check back with you on these direct quotes."

"Wait a minute," Mr. Forrester said as she stood. He made a few quick motions with a pencil. Karen couldn't see what he was doing because the drawing table was slanted out of her line of vision.

"Here's a little souvenir of the interview," he said, handing her a sheet of paper on which he had sketched a picture.

"Why, this is a drawing of me," she said delightedly.

"I'm glad you recognize it. It had to be a cartoon since I don't really know you well enough to do a portrait or a caricature."

"Thank you very much," she said, slipping it into her notebook so it wouldn't get wrinkled. "I've never had a sketch of myself. Usually I don't like to see my picture, but this is different."

Mr. Forrester glanced out of the window. "It's still raining," he said. "Why don't I take you and your mother home in my car, since we all go the same direction?"

"I'll ask Mother and see what she says," Karen replied, hoping Mother would consent.

"I'll go downstairs with you," he said. He buttoned his shirt collar and yanked a brilliant red tie from the back of a chair.

They got off the elevator and walked to the switchboard where Mother was waiting.

"Mother," Karen said. "This is our neighbor, Mr. Forrester."

Mr. Forrester said, "We've already met, Karen."

"Yes," her mother explained. "We met in the lobby of the apartment this morning. I couldn't get my umbrella opened, and Mr. Forrester helped me with it."

Mr. Forrester laughed good-naturedly and said, "I was a real help. I broke it. I should have known better than to fool around with it."

"It was worth a broken umbrella to get a ride to work,"

Mother said. "I don't care much for the rain. It was quite a surprise when I discovered that this was the Mr. Forrester you talked about so much this morning."

"A happy surprise, I might say," he added. "It's still raining, and I assume your umbrella is still broken. I'd like to drive you home."

"We'd be very grateful," Mother said.

As the car moved along the rain-slick street, Mr. Forrester cleared his throat and said, "I'd really like to repay you for breaking your umbrella. If you two don't have any special plans for dinner, I'd like to take you to a little restaurant I like."

"That's very nice of you," Mother said, "but I think you've repaid us sufficiently by taking us home."

"Let me be honest," Mr. Forrester said. "I really asked you to dinner because I don't enjoy eating by myself. I'd like your company."

Finally Mother smiled and said, "We'd enjoy going to dinner with you, Mr. Forrester."

The restaurant was in the basement of an old brick building. It was necessary to go down several steps to the entrance. At first Karen wondered what was so special about the place, but once they were inside, she felt as if she had entered another world.

The walls were all of red brick, and the floor was made of softly tinted flagstone. Small tables were covered with red-and-white-checked tablecloths. There were colored candles dripping wax onto the bottles in which they were anchored. The chairs were of white wrought iron, and baskets of ivy and red geraniums hung from the ceiling. A miniature fountain sprayed water which seemed to change colors when the lights played on it.

Karen's eyes couldn't seem to move fast enough to take

it all in. As the maître d'hôtel directed them to a table, Karen looked at the murals of scenes from Italy on the walls.

"It's just like eating in an outdoor restaurant in Rome," Karen breathed excitedly.

"This is one of my favorite haunts," Mr. Forrester said. "I've always wanted to travel. Someday I will, but right now I come to places like this and imagine far-away lands. Sometimes I go to the Patio for Mexican food, or to the Jade Gardens. That's a Cantonese restaurant."

Mr. Forrester ordered for them. Karen couldn't help noticing that the waiters treated him like an old friend.

Karen thought she had never laughed so much or enjoyed a meal more than she did that evening. They leisurely ate heaping platefuls of ravioli and lasagna sprinkled generously with Parmesan and Mozzarella cheeses. There was a spicy tossed salad and a basket of garlic bread.

"Now," said Mr. Forrester, "how about a big bowl of spumoni?"

Karen swallowed and said, "I don't think I can eat another bite of that hot spicy food."

"Spumoni is ice cream," Mr. Forrester informed her.

Mother smiled. "It does sound like a cross between macaroni and spaghetti."

"This is one of the most pleasant evenings I have had in a long time," Mr. Forrester said. "My wife, Martha, passed away three years ago. I don't enjoy going back to the apartment by myself in the evening. My son and daughter keep urging me to buy a trailer and take that trip to Mexico I keep talking about, but. . . ." He stopped talking, and absentmindedly turned the salt shaker over and over in his hand. "Well, it's not much fun to go places alone. They seem to lose all their meaning when you can't share

94

new places and new experiences with someone you care for."

Edna Beal looked at her watch. "My goodness, it's almost eight o'clock," she said. "I think we'd better be getting home. I'm sure Karen has homework to do."

Mr. Forrester parked his car in front of the apartment house. "Thanks again for a nice evening. We'll have to do this again some time."

"Thank you," Mother said. "It has been delightful."

"Yes, thanks," Karen said, leaning over to speak through the car window. "Thanks for dinner and the interview and the drawing."

Karen and her mother had started up the steps to the building when they heard several brief honks behind them. They turned.

"Mrs. Beal," Mr. Forrester called. "I'll drive you to work again tomorrow morning."

Mother seemed at a loss for words. Then she called back, "I usually walk." She paused. "But I'd appreciate a ride if it's raining."

In the elevator on the way to their apartment, Karen said, "Isn't he just the greatest?"

She opened her notebook and showed her mother the pencil sketch he had made of her that afternoon during the interview. "Wait until Jennie sees this."

The elevator stopped, and they got off and walked down the hall to their apartment. As Mother opened the door, she said, "I think it will be all right for you to plan on going up to Northwood. Mr. Forrester told me this morning that it is really quite a nice event and well chaperoned."

"Oh, Mother," Karen shrieked. She tried to hug her mother, but succeeded mainly in dropping all her books in the hallway. "I love you, Mother."

"Shhhhh," Mother cautioned. "Don't forget, we've got neighbors to think about."

That night, as Karen was twisting her hair onto large pink rollers, she talked excitedly about The Invite. Her mother looked through the mail.

"Karen," Mother said, "I'm afraid I won't be able to get any new clothes for you to take on the trip. You'll have to manage with what you have in the closet."

Karen said, "Don't worry about a thing. I'll take care of the clothes problem. Jennie is going to make her dress. She says she can do it for a third the cost of something ready made."

"We can't even afford material right now. I have some unexpected expenses." Mother held up an envelope. "The hospital has just informed me that they made a mistake in billing me. It seems I owe them more money."

Karen started to suggest that Dad should help pay for some of the hospital expenses, but she remembered that Mother hadn't responded favorably to that kind of suggestion before.

"We'll make out," Karen said, trying to sound hopeful.

The more Karen thought about her dad, the more she was convinced that he would provide the solution to her problem of new clothes. After all, he lived by himself now. He didn't have the expense of maintaining a family. She'd call him tomorrow and ask him for money to buy material to make a new formal.

7.

The Trip to Northwood

THE Friday morning on which Jennie and Karen were to travel to Northwood dawned with an uncertain aura about it. A heavy ground fog which lay over the city gave everything an unreal appearance. Karen felt as though she might be living in some temporary dream world which might suddenly evaporate if she did not tread carefully.

Some disquieting incidents had occurred as Karen got ready for this weekend. When she called Dad and asked if he would give her the money to buy material for a new formal, he seemed reluctant. She tried to explain to him that she was just trying to save money by not buying a ready-made dress. He said, noncommittally, that he would think it over.

Karen was annoyed and hurt. It didn't seem fair for him not to feel any responsibility for her. It seemed to Karen that Dad ought to be willing to provide something for his daughter. According to Mother, the small amount he was required by law to pay for her care wasn't sufficient.

After she talked to him on the phone, Karen stood in the lobby of the apartment house, trying to control the tears of frustration that persisted.

The next day after school Karen discovered her dad waiting for her in his car by the bus stop. He explained that he'd had a change of plans, and wanted her to have a new dress after all. He drove her downtown and insisted that she select a dreamy confection of cerulean blue chiffon. As if that weren't enough, he insisted on purchasing a pair of slim jims and a matching shell blouse in a brilliant orange sherbet shade for her to wear to the picnic.

Karen was then faced with the problem of how to pack the new clothing without letting her mother see it, and thereby eliminate the need for embarrassing explanations. Karen solved that dilemma rather neatly, she thought. She arranged to have the department store deliver the new clothes to Jennie Simmons' house.

When Dad took Karen home from the shopping trip, Karen suggested that he let her out a block away from the apartment house so there would be no danger of having Mother confront the two of them together. Dad seemed only too glad to do this.

"Have a wonderful time up at Northwood," Dad said, before he drove away from the corner. "This will be a weekend to remember for a long time."

He reached out and pressed something into her hand. As the car pulled away from the curb, Karen looked down and saw that she was holding a crumpled five-dollar bill. She shook her head slightly and breathed deeply. Sometimes parents could be extremely complicated to understand.

To make the situation even more involved, the day before Mother had come home late from work. She handed Karen a large gray box with imposing Old English lettering in maroon which proclaimed that this was a Longman's purchase. Karen gasped. Longman's was one of the best stores in town. Karen took a deep, nervous breath before she opened the box and looked inside. On a bed of tissue paper lay a crisply tailored pink linen suit.

"I'm sorry I couldn't afford to get a new formal for you," Mother said, "but I thought you ought to have something new for such a special trip. This will be nice for the concert and for church."

Karen's stomach churned with a mixture of uncomfortable feelings. She was deeply touched at this expression of Mother's love.

Karen held the suit up in front of herself and walked over to the mirror. Deep in her heart, she felt she hadn't been quite fair with her mother. She wondered if she should reveal the entire story on the clothes. Mother could return the suit to the store and get her money back if she wished. Karen turned to her mother, but something made her decide not to tell about the formal and the sportswear.

"It's a beautiful suit, Mother. I don't know how to thank you," she said.

"Have a good time, honey," Mother answered. "That's all the thanks I want."

Now, this Friday morning, Karen hurriedly dressed in her blue skirt and sweater from Christmas. It would be suitable for both school and the train trip to Bluffton.

She examined her suitcase once more to make sure she had everything. She decided that, no matter how terrible she looked, she'd have to wear her hair in curlers until she got to school. If she combed it out now, the fog would take the curl out in fifteen minutes.

When Karen went into the kitchen to help fix breakfast, she was surprised to see that Mother had it all prepared. In addition, there was a tantalizing aroma issuing from the utility counter, where Mother was icing a cake. Karen couldn't remember when her mother had last done any baking. It was good to see her humming happily as she swirled the gooey chocolate frosting on the top layer.

"Go ahead and eat, Karen," her mother said. "I want to finish this cake so you can take it with you. It's for Cliff. I'll put it in this old hatbox and tie it with string to make it easier for you to carry."

Karen quailed inwardly. It was going to be difficult enough to get across town on the bus with her suitcase and school books, without adding a cake in a hat box to her load. Karen started to object, but she thought somewhat guiltily of the new pink suit Mother had sacrificed to buy for her.

As she got ready to leave, Karen thought for a moment that her mother was going to cry, so she quickly brushed Mother's cheek with a kiss and hurried out into the hallway.

"I've got to run, or I'll miss that bus."

Karen pushed the elevator button with her elbow. When the car quivered to a stop at her floor and the door slid open, she found herself face to face with Mr. Forrester.

"Well, well," he said in his booming big voice. "Are you going on safari or running away to join the foreign legion?"

"I guess it looks like it," Karen acknowledged. "I'm going up to Northwood State College right after school for the weekend."

"Oh, The Invite," Mr. Forrester said, nodding. "I went up there a couple of times when my son and daughter were in school. You wait for me in the lobby," he directed. "I'll drive my car around to the front door and load this stuff up. I'll drive you to school."

"That's very nice of you," Karen said gratefully, "but I can't let you go clear across town."

"Give me your suitcase and hatbox," he commanded.

"It may look like a hatbox," she said, handing it to him,

"but there's a cake in it. Mother baked it for my brother, Cliff, who's up at Northwood."

"Lucky Cliff," he said, holding the box gingerly. "I haven't tasted homemade cake in ages."

Karen filed that in the back of her mind. It would be a nice way to repay Mr. Forrester for all the favors he had done for her.

By the time school was dismissed that afternoon, and Jennie's dad had unloaded the girls and their luggage at the station, the sun had come out and was shining. It had tinted everything with a golden veneer.

"What a weekend this is going to be!" Karen said happily, as they boarded the train and located seats.

Jennie yawned, and Karen laughed. "How casual can a person get? Here I'm shaking with excitement, and you're yawning as though you did this every day."

"Mom and I were up until two o'clock this morning hemming my formal," Jennie explained, and then she yawned again. She snuggled up in the far corner of the seat.

Karen opened her history book with good intentions of studying, but she couldn't keep her thoughts on westward expansion or "Manifest Destiny." Her fingers felt the money Mother had pinned inside her pocket. She smiled to herself. That was typical of Mother. Dad always used to say that Mother was nothing but a worrywart.

Karen used to think of things like that as jokes between the two of them. Now she wondered if there hadn't been a deeper significance to the jocular criticisms. How many times had she failed to understand the bitterness behind the things they said to one another in a bantering manner? Karen shook her head.

Jennie woke up and stretched when the porter went

101

through the car ringing the bell announcing the first call for dinner.

"Mom packed a lunch for us so we wouldn't have to spend all our money in the diner," Jennie said. "Are you hungry?"

The girls bought cartons of milk at the snack bar, and then devoured the fried chicken, potato salad, carrot sticks, and deviled eggs. After they had eaten, Karen noticed Jennie digging through the lunch bag.

"What's the matter?" Karen asked. "Did you lose something?"

"I was sure Mom put some cookies in for us, but I can't find them. Maybe she was so groggy after staying up late last night that she forgot them."

Karen thought of the money Dad had given her.

"I'll tell you what," Karen said. "Let's go to the diner for dessert. I'll treat."

"Are you sure it's okay?" Jennie asked. "I don't want you to be short of funds this weekend."

"My Dad gave me a little extra money, and so did Mother."

"Lucky you," Jennie said, "to have two sources of income. I have to settle for one." Then Jennie looked a bit embarrassed, as she realized what she had said. "I didn't mean . . ." she started to apologize.

Karen said brusquely, "I hope we don't have to wait long to be seated in the diner."

Karen thought to herself that no matter how careful people were, they always blundered onto delicate areas of conversation. It was too bad that situations had to exist that forced people to walk mental tightropes, trying to avoid hurting someone else unintentionally.

Karen and Jennie made their way along the gently swaying aisles of the train. They went through several air-operated doors which whished shut perilously close behind them. They were giggling uncontrollably by the time they reached the dining car, and had to wait outside to regain their composure before entering.

"Let's live it up," Karen said. "Look, they're featuring strawberry upside-down cake. How about it?"

Jennie nodded.

They were just finishing their cake when the train pulled into the Bluffton station.

They hurried back to their seats to collect their belongings.

As the train chuffed to a stop, Jennie looked curiously out of the window. Karen scanned the platform. "There's Gary," she said excitedly, as she saw his dark crew cut.

"I don't see anyone with him. You don't suppose my date backed out, do you?" Jennie said, and Karen detected more than a slight nervousness in her voice.

"He's probably here, but if you don't know what he looks like, how can you recognize him?" It didn't make much sense when Karen said it, but Jennie seemed to be comforted. Suddenly, she grabbed Karen's arm tightly.

"There! See that tall boy with his back to us? He's got on a gray jacket. He's standing just to Gary's left. I wish he'd turn around. Maybe that's Bill."

Karen looked in the direction Jennie had indicated.

"I don't think so, Jennie. He seemed to be with that pretty blonde girl, so he couldn't be your date." Then Karen let out a whoop of recognition. "Hey, that's Cliff."

As they got off the train, Cliff and Gary hurried toward them. Cliff grabbed Karen and hugged her.

"Watch out," she warned. "You'll squash this." She held the hatbox toward him.

"You can always get another hat," he said, "but where can you get another brother like me?"

"That's a good question," Karen said. "However, this isn't a hat. It's a cake. Mother made it for you."

Karen turned to Gary. Now that she was actually here with him, she realized she didn't know quite what to say or do. So, she smiled.

"Gee, I'm glad you could come, Karen," he said. He took her suitcase.

Jennie relieved the awkward groping for words by asking, "Where's Bill? He didn't change his mind about me, did he?"

"Bill is waiting for us at the college dining room," Gary said. "He hustles dishes there. He couldn't get off work in time to meet the train."

"Let's load up," Cliff said impatiently. "I've got my car over there."

"Your car?" Karen asked in surprise. "When did you get a car?"

"It's a long story," Cliff said. He stopped and snapped his fingers. "Here, we've been standing and gabbing, and I forgot to introduce Sally to you girls."

Cliff led them to the blonde girl standing near the magazine rack outside the station.

"Karen and Jennie, this is Sally Miller. She's your hostess while you're here."

Karen thought she detected a proprietary note in Cliff's voice and manner.

Karen, Jennie, and Gary got into the back seat of Cliff's late-model blue Valiant. Karen watched Sally move close to the driver's side. It was strange that Cliff hadn't mentioned the new car or Sally in any of his letters home. But, come to think of it, he hadn't written many letters home lately.

At the college dining room they met Bill. He was a quiet fellow who wore dark-rimmed glasses. Karen felt that he was every bit as nervous about Jennie as she was about meeting him.

Bill directed them to a corner table, and disappeared into the kitchen. He returned carrying a tray loaded with huge slices of shortcake covered with unbelievably big strawberries. Each creation was topped with a glacier of whipped cream.

Bill grinned rather self-consciously. "The cook let me serve these up myself."

Karen and Jennie exchanged knowing glances. Karen didn't know how she would ever get it all eaten, but Bill seemed so pleased with the treat that she didn't have the heart not to try.

As Karen swallowed the last bite, Bill asked, "Does anyone want seconds?"

Jennie opened her mouth to protest, but Karen jammed an elbow into her sides.

"We still have to get dressed for the concert," Karen reminded them.

Sally took the girls to the dormitory room where they were to stay.

"If there's anything you need, let me know." Then she paused, and looked closely at Karen. "Are you all right? You seem a bit pale."

Karen admitted that she didn't feel too well. Sheepishly, she told Sally about the double desserts.

"You two have time to lie down and rest for a while before the concert," Sally said. "Karen, I'll see if the dorm mother has something to settle your stomach."

Karen had never appreciated classical music very much, but tonight it took on an entirely new significance for her. She felt drawn into the very soul of the composer as the woodwinds and strings began the wistful sounds of Tchaikovsky's *Romeo and Juliet*. In the darkened auditorium she felt a warm hand close over hers. She didn't dare look toward Gary, but she returned the brief moment of pressure. As the music filled her ears, she recognized the plaintive cry of the violins which were playing the melody more familiar to her as "None but the Lonely Heart." Here, with the music, she felt a closeness to Gary which she could not communicate with words.

After the concert, Gary asked, "Would you like to go to the Student Union? We can dance there, or play Ping-Pong."

She shook her head. "No, thank you. The concert was so perfect, I don't want to spoil the memory of it."

"Let's just walk around then," Gary suggested.

As they strolled hand in hand, the most ordinary things about the campus seemed to assume a magic appearance. She didn't speak, and Gary didn't either. Karen was glad for the silence. She didn't want ordinary words to interfere and break the spell.

When they reached the dormitory porch, they paused. Karen wondered what Gary was thinking. She had imagined what it would be like to have Gary kiss her good night. She had always believed that a kiss should be something very special, not given freely to anyone as payment for a date. It ought to mean that two people care for each other very much. She cared for Gary, but she hoped he wouldn't kiss her unless he really cared for her.

As they stood together in the cool evening air, two familiar figures came up the dark. They were holding hands and talking quietly. It was Cliff and Sally.

When Cliff saw Karen and Gary standing by the steps, he said, "Well, Sis, how would you like some of that cake Mother sent me? Or would you prefer another helping of strawberry shortcake?"

He and Sally laughed and went into the dormitory lounge.

Karen was glad that it was dark so that Gary couldn't see her face. She was certain she was blushing—blushing at the thought that Sally and Cliff had had a laugh at her expense. She felt like a silly little girl who had eaten too much and had gotten sick. She wondered if Cliff would tell Gary about it later in the evening.

Gently Karen pulled her hand from Gary's.

"I'm kind of tired, Gary. It was a long train ride. Thanks so much for the concert. It was wonderful. I'll see you tomorrow morning."

Jennie wasn't in the room when Karen went upstairs. Karen got into her blue robe, and started rolling up her hair as she waited.

Mentally Karen scolded herself. Why did she let little things upset her so much? It had been a perfect day. Then she had let a chance remark by her big brother ruin a wonderful evening. She shouldn't really care what he said or did. So what if he did laugh at her? What if Gary laughed, too? But she didn't think he would. Gary wasn't that way.

But Cliff had ruined that quiet moment when she had been with Gary. Karen knew she was a lot like her mother. Everything had to be storybook-perfect. Grandmother had said that life wasn't all music and flowers. She knew she had better quit being so sensitive about little things, or she'd lose Gary. Lose him? She wasn't even certain she had him to lose. Gary wasn't going to be interested for long in a

107

girl who changed her mood with every wind that blew.

It was almost forty-five minutes later when Jennie breezed into the room where Karen was.

"I thought I was going to have to send out a St. Bernard to rescue you," Karen said, and it didn't sound as cheerful as she wished it had.

Jennie laughed and flopped across the bed. Karen felt a bit hurt that there was obviously some joke she had not been in on.

"You'll never believe it," Jennie howled. "Do you know where that idiot Bill wanted to take me?"

Jennie didn't wait for Karen to answer. "He wanted to go back to the dining room and get another piece of strawberry shortcake." Jennie dissolved into another spasm of laughter. "How can a guy who eats like that stay so skinny? I thought he was shy and quiet when I first met him, but he's a riot."

Karen felt an unwanted stab of jealousy. Jennie seemed to have so much fun everywhere she went. Nothing ever seemed to perturb her.

Jennie stopped laughing and rolled over on her side. "Listen," she said.

Karen paused, puzzled at the sound of music which seemed to be coming from outside their window. She shrugged and said, "I think someone must have a radio on too loud."

There was a quiet tap on their door, and Sally stuck her head inside. "Hurry and turn out your lights," she said, "and go to the window."

"What is it?" Karen asked.

"See for yourselves," Sally invited, opening the curtains.

Karen flipped off the bed lamp, and the girls made their way carefully across the darkened room and looked outside.

On the quadrangle of lawn below them stood shadowy forms, lighted only by flickering candles.

"The men are serenading us," Sally explained.

Karen leaned on the window sill and closed her eyes as the deep voices floated upward through the crisp night air.

One song blended right in with the next. They sang, "The Sweetheart of Sigma Chi" and "Always." Then they harmonized on "Someone Like You" and "Girl of My Dreams." As the deep sounds filled the air, Karen had the crazy sensation that she could distinguish Gary's voice from the rest. He seemed to be singing just to her. Gradually the serenaders faded away into the darkness, leaving the notes of "Goodnight Sweetheart" still in Karen's ears.

Neither Karen nor Jennie spoke, but finished getting ready for bed without turning on the light again. Karen pulled the cool sheets up over her and closed her eyes. She wondered if she could really be the kind of girl a fellow like Gary would care for. If only she could shake off the problems that had depressed her for the past several months, maybe she could be herself again. But was it fair to blame her moodiness on problems? No one had life just exactly as she wanted it. Tomorrow she would make a new start. No matter what happened, she would be bright and gay and lots of fun.

8.

A Startling Surprise

On Saturday morning, Karen awoke long before the small alarm went off. She went down the hall and showered, and then came back to the room to dress. She put on the new orange blouse her dad had bought her, but decided to save the slim jims for the picnic later. She thought her brown pleated skirt might be more appropriate, since Gary had told her they would be touring some of the classroom exhibits on campus that morning.

Jennie was still in bed when Karen heard a whistle under their window, followed by a small shower of pebbles bouncing off the glass. She raised the window and looked out. Gary was waving to her from the grassy area below.

"Bill had to get over to the dining room to work. He sent me to take you and Jennie to breakfast."

"We'll be down in a minute," Karen called.

After breakfast Gary took Karen to the biology lab to show her some experimental plants he was growing without soil. She tried to ask intelligent questions even though she didn't really understand half of what he was talking about. She was interested because of his dedication to the project. She thought of what a useful person Gary was going to be. She wasn't certain just what, if anything, she would ever contribute to the good of society.

After Karen peered through microscopes and looked at charts until her eyes blurred, Gary snapped his fingers. "Here I am boring you with all this while there are still lots of other things to see."

Protesting that she wasn't bored, she let him hurry her outside.

"Would you be be interested in seeing some of the displays in the Home Economics building?" Gary asked.

Karen looked at him mischievously, and, detecting a typical male reluctance, she said, "Yes, I'd be very interested."

They consumed another hour looking at the various exhibits of clothing design and home planning.

Later, in the warm sunshine, they climbed the wooded hill in back of the campus where there was a small planetarium.

"I suppose Cliff has brought you and your folks up here," Gary said.

"No, he hasn't," Karen said, thinking that she'd really seen very little of Northwood in spite of the fact that her brother was a student here. Mother and Dad had been so involved in the real estate business that they hadn't made many trips up to the school. The more Karen thought about it, the more she realized that Cliff never talked much about college when he was home for brief vacations.

"I wish it were evening," Gary said. "This is one of the nicest spots on the campus at night."

Karen looked at him out of the corner of her eye and said, teasingly, "Oh, do you come up here often?"

Gary grinned, "I meant that there's a lot to see up here at the planetarium—the stars, the moon."

"It's almost like being in a separate little world," Karen said, "where everything unpleasant can be shut out."

"I can't think of anything unpleasant right now," Gary said.

He took her by the shoulders and pulled her to him. She felt his lips on hers briefly. Then Gary put his arm about her waist, and they walked slowly back to the dormitory.

The warm sun felt good on her back as they walked along. She listened to the sound of the big clock in the bell tower as it chimed eleven. They hadn't been up on the hill for more than fifteen minutes, but it seemed like the best part of a lifetime to Karen.

As they approached the dorm, they could see the chartered buses in the parking lot.

"We'd better hurry," Gary said, "or we'll miss out on the picnic." Karen didn't really care if they missed the bus to the picnic.

As she dressed for the dance that evening, Karen was aware of the constant flow of activity in the dorm. Girls were dashing from room to room borrowing clothing and asking for help with zippers. It was fun to be in the midst of this kind of excitement. It was much better than dressing for a prom at home, alone.

After a series of minor crises, the worst being that Jennie had forgotten the shoes she usually wore with her formal and had had to borrow a pair of white flats which were a size too large, the girls went downstairs. Karen felt very regal as they went through the French doors which led into the women's lounge. The lounge itself was full of fellows waiting for their dates.

KAREN had never seen Gary in a white dinner jacket before. Her hands shook as she accepted the florist's box from him. She pulled off the ribbon which bound the box. In a bed of shredded cellophane lay a delicate white orchid.

"It's so lovely," Karen whispered.

"Just like the girl who is going to wear it. I'm glad your dress is blue. It's the same color as that skirt and sweater you wore at Christmas, isn't it?"

Karen nodded and smiled, pleased that he should have noticed and remembered.

The Student Union had been transformed into a circus. There were twisting mobiles fashioned like circus acrobats and high wire artists, each on its own silvery trapeze. Cardboard cutouts of clowns, bareback riders, and performing animals lined the walls. Refreshment tables around the outside of the dance floor had canopied styrofoam merry-go-rounds as centerpieces. Large nets, which had been coated with gilt paint and gold glitter, held brightly colored balloons above the heads of the dancers.

The master of ceremonies, who was dressed as a ring master, complete with a red-sequined jacket, white trousers, highly polished black boots, and a tall silk hat, signaled the band leader to start the music.

Gary and Karen danced until the band began to play La Raspa. They lasted only a few rounds, and finally had to find their table and watch other couples gradually leave the floor.

Across the room Karen saw Cliff and Sally returning to their table. Karen's eyes widened in surprise. She wasn't sure her brain was accurately recording what she saw. A man sitting at the table with her brother looked like Dad.

"Let's go over and say 'hello' to Cliff and Sally," Karen suggested.

Gary took her arm and led her through the small groups of talking, laughing people. As they neared Cliff's table, Karen realized with a feeling of inexplicable apprehension that the man actually was Dad. He didn't see her at first, but when he did, he stood up quickly.

"Karen! How pretty you look! That dress is just right for you."

He turned to a woman sitting at the table with him.

"Clara," he said, "this is my daughter, Karen. Karen, I'd like you to meet Clara Allison."

"How do you do," Karen said. "Dad, I think you know Gary Simmons."

"Yes, I remember Gary," he said, and shook hands with him. "Good to see you again. Possibly you know Miss Allison?"

Gary grinned and said, "'I guess almost everybody at Northwood knows you, Miss Allison." He explained to Karen, "Miss Allison is head of the business office."

"Well," Dad said, awkwardly, "there's the music again. I suppose you young people don't want to miss a single dance. So, don't let me keep you here talking to me."

Karen had the distinct feeling she was being dismissed.

Gary asked Karen, "How about it? This sounds a little more relaxed than *La Raspa*."

As they danced, Karen's eyes moved back curiously to the table where her dad and Miss Allison sat talking. She wondered why her dad hadn't mentioned that he was coming up to Northwood for The Invite.

Finally, Karen said aloud, "I wonder where Miss Allison's date is?"

"Probably doesn't have one," Gary said. "She's here as a chaperon, I think."

Later in the evening, Karen saw her dad dancing with Miss Allison. It bothered her. She'd never seen Dad dance before, not even with Mother. It never occurred to her that he knew how to dance. He was probably only being polite, she told herself.

At last she could stand it no longer, and said, "Gary, would you mind asking Sally to dance? I'd like to talk to Cliff for a while."

Karen let Cliff circle her around the dance floor a couple of times before she asked, "Cliff, why didn't Dad tell me that he was coming up here this weekend?"

"He wasn't sure he was going to be able to come until the last minute. He telephoned me this morning and said that he was driving up to look at some property in the northern part of the state. I suggested that he stop over tonight and stay with me in the dorm."

"He knew I was going to be here at Northwood," Karen exclaimed, frowning. "I wonder why he didn't get in touch with me? I probably wouldn't have even known he was here if I hadn't seen him myself and gone over to speak to him."

Cliff didn't answer.

"Dad comes up here to see you quite often, doesn't he?" Karen continued.

"Look, Karen," Cliff said. "Things are pretty rough for Dad. He's lonely. Why shouldn't he come up here? He never had time before."

"He doesn't make much of an effort to visit me," she said petulantly.

"It's not easy to see you. It creates problems. If he calls or comes to see you at the apartment he runs the risk of having to talk to Mother. Neither of them wants that."

Karen knew it was true, but she pressed the point.

"We could arrange to visit each other away from the apartment."

"You always manage to contact him if you need something," Cliff said. "You know that it's not easy to meet him if Mother knows where you're going. She kicks up a fuss whenever his name is mentioned."

"You make it sound as if it's all Mother's fault," Karen said, defensively. "There are two sides to every story."

"That's exactly what I'm trying to get you to understand."

"The thing I don't understand is that Dad doesn't have any trouble arranging to see you, but he can't even visit with me when we live right in the same town. I don't think he cares very much what happens to me."

"That's not true and you know it," Cliff exploded.

"Don't yell at me like that," Karen demanded.

"Well, try to grow up and see things from someone else's point of view for a change," he growled.

"Maybe it's time somebody saw things from my point of view," Karen snapped. "People haven't worried about my feelings for a long time. They've just shoved me around to suit their own convenience."

"It hasn't been very convenient for any of us." Karen knew that Cliff was becoming extremely annoyed with her. "But we've got to learn to live with it," he said.

"That's a great thing for you to say," Karen accused. "You haven't had to live with it. You're hidden away up here where you don't have to be torn apart, but I don't have a hiding place."

Karen happened to glance over at the table where her dad had been sitting. She saw him stand and help Miss

Allison with her wrap. The two of them left together.

"Cliff," Karen said, dismayed at what she was thinking. "Is Dad here at the dance with Miss Allison? I mean, did they have a date?" It was so incredible she could hardly believe what she asked.

"Miss Allison was to be a chaperon, so I suggested Dad come along, too," Cliff said. "Clara's a very nice person, but she's very lonely."

"I can see why," Karen said. "She's not exactly the prettiest girl in town, is she?"

Karen felt Cliff's arm stiffen against her back. "If we weren't here on the dance floor, I'd give you the spanking you've deserved for a long time," he said through gritted teeth. "You're a spoiled brat. No wonder Dad comes up here to get away from all the unpleasantness."

Cliff stopped dancing and led Karen back to the table. They sat in sullen silence. She wanted to lash out and hurt him—hurt him the way he and Dad had hurt her.

Karen looked at Cliff and said, "Now I know where you got the new car. It explains why Dad bought me those expensive new clothes. He had to cover up his guilt for neglecting me."

"Just keep it up," he said. "Twist everything to suit yourself."

When Gary and Sally returned to the table, Cliff stood and said, "Here's your date back, Gary, old buddy. You're welcome to her with my compliments."

Karen thought Gary seemed confused by the exchange. As they walked away from Cliff and Sally, Karen had difficulty controlling her voice.

"Gary, would you mind taking me back to the dormitory?"

Gary was concerned. "Are you ill, Karen?"

Karen pressed her lips together tightly to keep her mouth from quivering. The tears of hurt and anger were very close to the surface. She had to get out of this place.

As they moved toward the doorway, there was a roll of drums, and the nets overhead were released. Cascades of balloons floated over them. Everyone surged forward to grab one. She could hear them popping here and there. Karen pushed frantically through the crowd to the door. She ran down the steps of the Student Union. Her shoes made a mocking sound in her ears. She could hear her mother accusing her of running away whenever the going got rough. She ran along the walk that led across campus to the dorm. She could hear Gary behind her. She ran faster. She didn't want him to see her like this. How could she explain what was wrong?

"Wait, Karen," he called.

When he caught up with her, he grabbed her arm and turned her toward him. "Karen, what's the matter?"

She ducked her head and tried to hold back the sobs. He put his hand under her chin and lifted her face to his.

"Karen," he said in surprise. "You're crying. Did I do something wrong? Did I say something to hurt you?"

She shook her head. "It isn't your fault."

He dug into his pocket and handed her a clean white handkerchief. When she had wiped her eyes, she said, "Gary, I'm so sorry. It seems as though all I do lately is apologize for my actions and moods, but so many things have happened that I can't quite understand or explain. . . ." She wasn't making sense, she knew.

"You don't have to explain anything to me, Karen," he said, "unless you want to talk about it."

They walked across the cool, quiet campus.

When they reached the dormitory steps, they paused

where they had the other night. Karen wished she could turn the clock back and relive the last several hours. She wished she could change the way she acted and the way she felt.

"Here," Gary said. "I almost forgot." He reached into his coat pocket. "I got a balloon for you, but I'm afraid I popped it." He held out the shriveled red balloon.

She took it and smiled. "This is what I did to your weekend," she said apologetically.

"Look at the balloon more closely," he said. "You didn't ruin my weekend."

He held the balloon up where she could see it better. Tied to the balloon was a gold ring, the kind won on a merry-go-round. He broke the string with which it was tied to the balloon and handed the ring to her.

Karen held it in the palm of her hand and looked at it. It was strange how this could make her forget all the brass rings life had been handing her lately.

9.

A Door Opens

KAREN was surprised when Mr. Simmons took her home from the train station on Sunday evening to find the apartment locked. Mother didn't answer when she called at the door. A moment of panic swept over Karen as she remembered those terrible days back in December when her mother was so depressed and ill. Her hands shook as she fumbled through her purse looking for her door key. Suppose something had happened? Her mother had been ready to cry when Karen had left on Friday morning. Perhaps Mother had become terribly lonely in the apartment by herself with Karen gone for the weekend. Maybe she had . . . Karen shrank from her thoughts.

She hurried to the elevator and pushed the button that took her to the first floor. She went to the door of the manager's apartment and rang the bell. There was no response. The television was on inside and turned up very loud. Desperately Karen knocked on the door several times. Each time she pounded a bit louder and more urgently. Her knuckles tingled.

When the manager did come to the door, he looked at her impatiently.

"What's the matter this time?" he growled.

"I've forgotten my door key," Karen stammered.

"Okay," said the manager crossly, and reached behind the door where he kept a master key. "When you bring this back, stick it under my door. I don't want to miss any more of Ed Sullivan than I have already."

Karen glared back at him. He was obviously more interested in television than he was in doing his job. Her mother might be ill or something worse, but of course, he couldn't know that.

She ran back to the elevator, but someone had called it upstairs. Frantically she pushed the button, but it was so slow making its descent that she ran to the service stairs and raced up all three flights.

"Mother," she called, once inside. A lamp on the corner end table lighted the room, but there was no one around. Quickly she went to the bedroom. It was empty. Karen looked in the bathroom. No one there either. The same in the kitchen. Where could Mother be? Then Karen noticed a piece of paper on the kitchen table. She snatched it up. It was a note for her:

> Karen: Welcome home! Hope you had a marvelous time. I'll be home late. Don't wait up. Phil Forrester and I have gone out to dinner and then to an art exhibit. If you're hungry, there is a TV dinner in the refrigerator.
>
> Love,
> Mother.

The note fluttered to the floor as Karen sank down on a chair with relief. She couldn't help wondering if she'd ever get over her fear that Mother would do something foolish if she became despondent again.

Karen went into the bedroom. She unpacked everything in her suitcase except the new formal and the sports outfit Dad had bought her. She wished she had the nerve to explain to her mother how she had acquired these clothes so that she could wear them again. For now, however, she left them in the suitcase and put it at the back of the closet.

She intended to read her history lesson as she soaked in a hot bath, but history didn't have a chance against the thought of the weekend and Gary.

Karen slipped into her robe and slippers while she rolled up her hair. Then she sat down at the kitchen table and started a letter to Gary. There were many things she wanted to tell him, but it wasn't easy to put down on paper how much she appreciated the way he had accepted her problems without prying questions. She liked the way he seemed to understand that there were hurts inside that she couldn't talk about. She rewrote it a dozen times, but somehow, it didn't ever come out quite the way she wanted it to.

Karen went to bed. As a last thought, she put the gold ring under her pillow.

When Karen heard her mother come in, she looked sleepily at the clock. It was almost midnight.

On Monday, at school, Karen's speech teacher told her that the local TV station wanted a student to represent Marshall High School on the Teen Town program. Karen was to be prepared to discuss, "A teen-ager's place in today's world." She would be on a panel with students from other schools.

Wednesday afternoon, Karen entered the Humbolt Building, where the television studio WXMW was located. She asked the woman at the desk in the small outer office where she was expected to go for the Teen Town program.

"You're early," the receptionist said. "Just sit over there. When the other panel members come, you can all go to the studio together."

Karen was glad for the extra time. She wanted to look over her notes again and be certain she knew what she was going to say. She didn't have long, however, for another girl soon came in and sat down by Karen.

"I'm Elizabeth Little," said the newcomer. "I go to Central."

"I'm Karen Beal from Marshall. Are you here for the Teen Town show?"

The girl nodded. "Are you as nervous as I am?"

Karen realized that she'd been too preoccupied with other things to really think about getting scared. But once Elizabeth had mentioned it, she began to feel the fluttering sickness in her stomach that went with stage fright.

"I couldn't even eat lunch today," Elizabeth confessed.

Karen wished the girl would stop talking about it. She was making it worse for both of them.

Much to Karen's relief, two boys came into the room, accompanied by an overweight little man wearing a rumpled searsucker suit. His tie was loosened at the neck, and he had stuck the ends of it in one of his shirt pockets. In one hand he had a sheaf of papers which he waved and pointed with as he talked. Karen had the impression that he never moved at any speed slower than a gallop.

"Is he the announcer?" Karen whispered to Elizabeth.

"Goodness, no," Elizabeth returned. "The announcer is Ray Harrison." Elizabeth's tone indicated that Mr. Harrison was something special.

"Are these all the kids for the panel?" the messy little man asked the girl at the desk.

She nodded pleasantly.

"Okay, kids, I want you to listen closely," said the little man, waggling the papers at them. "You'll find placards with your names on them at the table inside. Find your places and sit down. The main thing is to speak clearly and slowly, but say whatever you please. Let's go.

"Here's your gang, Ray," he said. "You take it from here."

As Karen stepped inside the barnlike room, she saw a tangle of cameras, lights, and electrical cords. In the midst of this jungle a young man was sitting at a long table. He looked up and smiled when the door swung open. He was a complete contrast to the man who had greeted them.

Elizabeth whispered excitedly in Karen's ear, "Wow, he's even better looking in person than he is on TV. Isn't he dreamy on Platter Party?"

Karen shook her head. "I haven't had much time for television lately," she said.

"You're kidding!" Elizabeth exclaimed in disbelief.

Karen had to admit that the young man at the table was extremely good-looking. He was meticulously dressed in a blue-and-gray-plaid sports jacket. He was wearing a pale blue shirt and a darker blue knit tie. He had brown curly hair and his eyes . . . Karen realized that she had been staring at him and turned away, embarrassed. She looked for her name card and sat down.

When everyone was in his place, the young man said, "Thank you so much for coming to be on Teen Town. I'm Ray Harrison. I hope you'll enjoy our visit this afternoon. Why don't we introduce ourselves and get better acquainted?"

Karen looked at each person who spoke. One of the boys was from a parochial school in town, and the other was from a county school at the edge of the city limits. Mr.

Harrison surprised Karen with the amount of firsthand information he had about each school.

He knew that Central had won the county basketball tournament. He knew several members of St. Anthony's debating team. He was impressed by the good showing Mill County School's cross-country track team had made that season.

When Karen identified herself, he said, "Marshall's *Town Crier* is one of the best school papers in the state. You're editor of the feature page, aren't you?"

Karen relaxed as he chatted with them. Karen appreciated the fact that he didn't talk down to them, but treated them as intelligent persons with ideas to share.

"I read something in a magazine a few weeks ago," Mr. Harrison said. "It disturbed me because I felt there was an element of truth about it, and yet I thought perhaps it didn't reveal the complete picture of our youth.

"In Japan and France, and even in some of the newer African nations, students are very much involved in the political life of their countries. They seem to be aware of the critical nature of the world situation, and they are reacting to it. They know that they want a better world for their generation and for generations to come. They aren't afraid to take a stand, make a protest, even sacrifice or risk their personal safety to bring about changes. On the other hand, American young people seem more interested in fast cars, going steady, and rock 'n' roll. Most young Americans do not really know or even care what is going on in the world, or even in their own country, as long as they have plenty of spending money. They don't believe in anything. They have no cause except getting the most fun out of life."

He stopped reading and looked at them. "I think the

issue here is," he continued, " 'Are American teen-agers making any effort to be responsible persons in this world?' "

"That article," Elizabeth said, "makes us sound like a pretty soft bunch of jerks, but you've got to realize that we live in a different kind of society here in the United States. We have our freedom, and we can't help it because we have more money than these other countries. What is there for us to get excited about? What can we really do about the world situation, anyway?"

"Do you feel, then," Ray Harrison asked, "that we've 'got it made,' so to speak? Is there nothing in our country or government that needs changing? Is there nothing for young people to stand up and fight for?"

The boy from Mill County raised his hand. "No government is perfect, but ours seems to be better than most. Of course, there are things which ought to be changed, but some of us think there are ways of doing things other than starting rioting or having a revolution."

"That's not exactly the total picture of things," the boy from St. Anthony's objected. "There have been young people in this country who have joined sit-ins and other demonstrations to protest against injustices. And many kids are giving two years of their life to serve in the Peace Corps."

"But we can't join the Peace Corps until we're eighteen," Karen added, "and what percentage of American boys and girls have participated in sit-ins? We can't vote until we're twenty-one, in most states, so, actually we don't have too much to say about what is happening in this world."

"I think that's right," Elizabeth added. "Teen-agers can't really do anything unless their parents give permission. If we make suggestions, adults either ignore us or laugh at us. If we really did demonstrate the way they do in other countries, we'd have our pictures in the papers as juvenile delinquents."

The discussion continued back and forth. Karen found herself forced into a more pessimistic stand than she had wanted to take. She knew she was letting her resentment about her own situation affect her statements. She had almost forgotten the speech she had prepared for the program.

She tried to redeem herself by saying, "I suppose there are some positive ways young people can do something useful, but we aren't always aware of where we can help out. It may be that the most important thing we can do right now is to take advantage of the educational opportunities we have at school. We ought to learn all we can about the history of our country and how our government operates so that we can be informed citizens. We need to study and prepare ourselves to find useful work to do when we select a vocation."

"That may be a good note to end this discussion on," Ray Harrison said. "I want to thank you again for coming and sharing in this panel discussion. I'd like to present each of you with this gold pin to commemorate your participation."

He handed each of them a small pin shaped like a TV camera with gold letters WXMW.

He reached beneath the desk. "Here's a record album and a Longman's gift certificate for everybody."

"But when are we going to do the show?" the boy from St. Anthony's asked.

Mr. Harrison smiled. "We're all finished. You hardly felt any pain at all, did you?"

"Do you mean we've done the show already?" Karen exclaimed in surprise.

"That's right," he said. "We discovered a long time ago

that people tend to clam up once they know the camera is on them, so we decided to set this up like a preliminary get-acquainted period. We moved right into the program while we were all visiting. Later, we'll edit the tape, cut it down to the proper length, dub in the theme, add commercials and the rest of the necessities."

"I thought there was something strange going on," Elizabeth said. "I noticed that a red light flashed on that camera over there as soon as we sat down."

"I'm glad you didn't let it bother you," Mr. Harrison said. "You were all very natural and honest. Don't forget to have your parents and friends watch you when we run this tomorrow night at eight o'clock."

The panel members filed out of the studio, relieved that the ordeal was over. When everyone had left except Karen, she went into the small outer office.

"Is there a telephone I can use?" she inquired of the receptionist.

"Help yourself," said the girl with the red hair, motioning to a phone on her desk, "as long as it's a local call."

Karen dialed the number of her father's office. She wanted to tell him to be sure to watch the program tomorrow night. No one answered. She hung up disappointedly. He was hardly ever in the office anymore when she called.

Karen glanced at the wall clock. It was almost five o'clock. It wouldn't be long until Mother came to meet her.

She looked idly about the studio. There weren't any magazines which looked interesting. Then she noticed some drawings on the far wall and went over to see them more closely.

They were caricatures and Karen was sure she recognized the style. The first drawing showed the harried little man who had escorted the panel members into the studio. He was represented as the mythological Mercury with tiny wings on his feet. He was being launched for flight off a huge stack of papers. The drawing had captured his expression so perfectly that Karen almost laughed aloud. Another drawing was of the girl at the reception desk. The cartoonist had endowed the girl with a huge shock of red hair and a peppering of freckles. She was completely snared by a tangle of telephone cords. Karen didn't recognize the next two persons, but the last was obviously Ray Harrison. His handsome face peered out from a knight's helmet, and he was riding a little hobbyhorse on wheels.

"I see you're admiring our rogue's gallery."

Karen whirled and had a difficult time recovering her composure. Ray Harrison was smiling up at her from a wheelchair.

"These drawings were done by a good friend of mine," he said.

Karen managed to find her voice again in spite of her surprise.

"That's a coincidence," she said. "Mr. Forrester is my neighbor. He did a drawing of me, too."

"He's a great guy," Ray Harrison said.

Karen nodded.

"I'm surprised to find you still here," he said. "I thought everyone had gone."

"My mother is going to meet me here."

"I'm glad you're still here. I was going to call you tomorrow."

"Call me?"

"Yes. While we were doing the program, you said that young people would like to help others, but they didn't always know where they could be of service. I felt that you might be interested in a pet project of mine."

Karen wondered what he was going to suggest.

"Your voice has good timbre," he said. "Have you done any public speaking?"

"I belong to the Speech Club at school," Karen said, pleased at his compliment.

"I thought so," he said. "Are you interested in dramatics?"

"I guess I never really thought about that. Why?"

"I work with a group of young people who like to act. We do plays for children, stories like *Aladdin's Lamp* and *Alice in Wonderland*. We visit hospitals and children's homes. Sometimes we present them for the public. Then all the proceeds go to the Community Center. We have a great time together. We make all the sets and costumes ourselves."

"It sounds like fun," Karen said.

"We meet once a week. We're having a meeting this Friday evening at the Community Center. If you'd like to come, I'll see that you have transportation."

"I'd like to come, but I'll have to check with my mother."

"Good. Call the station here and let me know. If you can't get me, leave a message with Red over there." He looked at his watch. "I've got a newscast coming up. I'll have to go."

He wheeled the chair around with what Karen thought was amazing dexterity, and rolled through the swinging door.

THAT evening at home, as Karen was telling her mother all about her experiences at the station, Phil Forrester came over.

"I saw the drawing you did of Ray Harrison at the station," Karen said. "I didn't understand the wheels and the hobbyhorse until I discovered that he's in a wheelchair."

"It's strange the way people can change," Phil Forrester said. "Ray was in high school at the same time as my daughter. They even had a few dates. I didn't encourage it because he impressed me as one of the most unpleasant young men I had ever met. He was very conceited about his good looks and his talent as an actor. He'd had quite a bit of newspaper publicity. He was the home town boy that everyone was sure would make good in the big time some day. I wouldn't have dared draw a caricature of him at that time. He had no sense of humor about anything even vaguely connected with himself."

"He didn't act that way today," Karen said. "He was thoughtful, and seemed interested in helping us."

"That's the point I'm making. I don't think I have ever witnessed such a change as the one that occurred after Ray was in the accident. Oh, it didn't happen all at once. It was a long struggle. That accident was a terrible thing. His mother was driving him east for an audition around the first of March, about four years ago. It was late at night, and the roads were icy. She missed a curve. The car piled into a stone culvert and Ray was thrown out. He lay in the snow for hours before the police found him and his mother. He was in bad condition. He had broken his back, and the doctors said there was some nerve complication. In order to save his life, the doctors operated, but Ray was left crippled from the waist down."

"How terrible for him," Karen said. "What happened to his mother?"

"We all thought she was going to die. There was a time when some people thought death would have been a blessing for her. The worst part was knowing what had happened to Ray."

"I'm sure he didn't blame her," Karen said.

"That's where you're wrong," Mr. Forrester answered. "Ray was a very bitter young man. He often told his mother that he wished the accident had killed him instead of leaving him helpless. He felt that life held nothing for him, since he could no longer act. Most people cannot understand how seriously emotional problems can affect the human system."

"I can," Mother said, very softly. Karen glanced sympathetically at her mother. She was sure she knew what Mother was thinking.

"Ray's friends were convinced that he would be better off if he got a job. After much persuasion and many changes of his mind, Ray came to work in the copy room of the *Evening Dispatch*. He was able to do rewrite quite well. He began to receive a few assignments of his own, book reviews and things of that nature. Then someone hit on the idea of letting him review plays since he had a background in drama. This turned out to be a mistake. He wrote with bitter ink. His criticism of actors was so harsh that we often had to change his stories completely before printing them. Whenever he discovered a change, he flew into a terrible rage. He was taken off that assignment and put on rewrite again. He became increasingly despondent. He repeatedly resigned from his job. Finally the boss got fed up and let him quit. He said that Ray was hopeless."

Karen shook her head in disbelief. "It doesn't even sound like you're talking about the same person I met this afternoon."

"Who knows what might have happened to him if a local television station hadn't opened up about that time.

It was a small concern, working on a very limited budget. They couldn't afford much in the way of staff or announcers. Someone suggested to Ray that he ought to audition for a job there. He has a marvelously well-trained voice. At first he absolutely refused to consider it. I think he was afraid of failure. Frankly, the rest of us weren't so sure of his chances since his attitude was so negative. But the station manager was desperate, and several members of the *Dispatch* staff threw their weight around, so he was hired. The Community Center helped get him a car with hand controls so he would be a bit more independent. We all had our fingers crossed that he wouldn't muff this job."

Phil paused and took a drink of the lemonade Mother had served. Karen had a hunch she knew who the staff members on the *Dispatch* were who had helped Ray—at least she could guess one of them.

"One night the announcer had laryngitis," Mr. Forrester continued. "He couldn't go on with the eleven o'clock news. There was nothing to do but put Ray on. There was no time for temperament in an emergency like that. A desk and camera angles were arranged so that the wheelchair didn't show. He's still a little sensitive, but he makes a great show of bravado about it. Anyway, he was a bit shaky at first but he gained confidence as he became involved in the broadcast. A couple of days later he got three fan letters, two from girls who wanted to marry him and one from a speech professor at Northwood. Ray filled in on several other occasions. He proved so popular, especially with young people, that he graduated to a program of his own. Now, I think he has two—or is it three? Occasionally he puts on a special dramatic program featuring the group from the Community Center. As far as I know, he spends most of his spare time working for the Center. He's repaid them for that special car a dozen times over."

"I should imagine his mother is very proud of him," Mother said thoughtfully.

"Did Ray ever forgive her?" Karen asked.

Mr. Forrester leaned back comfortably in his chair and said, "I talked to Ray about that once. Ray told me that he never had to forgive his mother, because he realized that he was the one who needed forgiveness. He said he felt that somehow his life had been redeemed in a way he never could have planned."

"I don't think I understand completely," Karen said. "Do you mean he wasn't sorry that he couldn't go on the stage as he wanted to?"

"No, I think Ray will always love the stage, and he'll always wish he could have been a star. However, I think he has found out that what he had originally planned wouldn't have brought him the satisfaction or feeling of accomplishment he has now."

After Mr. Forrester had gone home, Karen started a letter to Gary. She wanted to share with him the kind of a person Ray Harrison was. The things Mr. Forrester had said fascinated her. The meaning of them was clarified in her mind as she wrote about them to Gary.

From the kitchen Karen could hear her mother humming cheerfully as she rinsed out the lemonade glasses. Karen thought how good it was to have Mother so happy.

10.

Crisis and Decision

AFTER school on Friday afternoon, Karen gratefully boarded the crowded, smelly city bus. She didn't even care that there wasn't a seat left. She was glad to have the school day ended. It had been unusually hectic. Marty Riffner had criticized what she had considered one of the best feature articles she had turned out for weeks. They had argued bitterly. He'd accused her of being more interested in activities up at Northwood than she was in Marshall's *Town Crier*. Karen had remarked snidely that he seemed unusually interested in things that didn't concern him.

Karen had almost quarreled with Jennie today, too. It all started because Jennie had planned a slumber party for that night.

"But Jennie, you knew I was planning to go that drama club meeting this evening," Karen said disappointedly.

"I forgot all about it," Jennie said.

Karen was hurt that Jennie evidently had asked everyone else before asking her. "Why didn't you call me last night when you thought about having a party?"

"I did call you," Jennie said, her eyes flashing. "At least

I tried to. I called the apartment phone, and the manager answered. He refused to go upstairs and call you to the phone. He said that he didn't have a phone for the benefit of two silly teen-age girls to talk on all night. That's the last time I call you, Karen Beal."

Jennie didn't get angry very often, but when she did, Karen knew enough to retreat carefully. Finally Jennie agreed to try to change the night, and told Karen so at the end of the day.

"Karen, I called Mom and she said we'd make a try on Saturday night this time. I talked to the other girls, and they agreed. Honestly, it wouldn't be any fun without you there. "

"Oh, Jennie," Karen said remorsefully. "I'm so sorry I snarled at you. I was off-balance from something else that happened. Marty Riffner was his usual obnoxious self today."

"It's okay, Karen. I understand," Jennie said.

Later, going home, Karen worried. How long would Jennie continue to understand? How long would people keep making excuses for her? Karen didn't like being the way she was. She knew she was overly sensitive and easily angered, but everything kept getting mixed up, just when she thought she had things straightened out. Nothing was right or normal anymore. She couldn't put her finger on any one thing, it was everything in general. It was the whole situation. She was tired of riding the city bus to school every day, but she couldn't bear the thought of changing to Central. She was tired of the crowded little apartment where she couldn't entertain her friends. She was tired of the feeling of impermanence, as though she and her mother were living in some sort of suspended animation, waiting for something to happen.

Perhaps things would be better after graduation. One more year, and then she'd be out on her own, as Cliff was.

Thinking of Cliff turned out to be a coincidence. When Karen walked into the front lobby of the apartment, he was there sprawled on one of the tattered old armchairs.

"Cliff!" she exclaimed. "What are you doing here? When did you get here? Have you seen Mother?" The questions tumbled from Karen's lips.

"Simmer down to a rolling boil and I'll answer you," Cliff said, standing up and picking up a suitcase. "Have you got a key to the apartment? I tried to get the manager to let me in but I guess he thought I'd steal all your jewels. I've been waiting about an hour," Cliff complained. "Dad drove me down."

"Dad?" Karen said in surprise.

"Yes, he's been up north all week working on a business deal. It's really something. Wait until you hear."

They got off the elevator and Karen unlocked the door of the apartment. Cliff went inside and headed straight for the kitchen.

"That's why I'm here," Cliff said.

Karen stood in the kitchen doorway as Cliff rummaged around in the refrigerator.

"Dad wants us to go out for dinner with him tonight," he said, "so hurry and put on your best bib and tucker. He'll pick us up at 5:30."

"I can't go," Karen said. "I have other plans."

"You're kidding," Cliff said, putting a jar of olives on the table.

"Is that so strange? Do you think nobody would ask your poor little ugly sister to go out?"

"I didn't mean that," Cliff said, munching on a chicken

leg. "I just thought you'd be home since Gary is up north. I thought you two had some sort of agreement."

Karen didn't answer, but wondered if the gold merry-go-round ring meant more than she allowed herself to think it did.

"Can't you change your plans?"

"No," Karen said, uncooperatively. "I've got a drama club meeting. I've been invited to join by the star of a television program." Karen didn't add that the star was known locally only.

Cliff stared at her incredulously. "What about tomorrow night?"

"I'm busy then, too. I'm going to a slumber party at Jennie's."

"Oh, that's nothing," Cliff said. "You girls can do that anytime."

"No, we can't," Karen said, watching Cliff pour a glass of milk. "Jennie changed the party until tomorrow night so I could be there. I can't ask her to change it again."

"Be reasonable for a change," Cliff pleaded. "It's important to Dad that we be with him tonight."

"Listen, Clifford Edward Beal," she said through tightened lips. "You never even gave a thought to what my plans might be. You marched in here without any warning and demanded that I do whatever you say. If I don't change my plans and do what you wish, then I'm unreasonable. I'm tired of being cast as the villain in every act. Did it ever occur to you that I might have some feelings?"

Cliff put the glass of milk on the kitchen drainboard and grabbed her arms. Karen thought he was going to shake her. Instead he hugged her.

"Sis, I'm sorry. I don't like to have this barrier between us all the time. I was disappointed that the three of us couldn't be together tonight. I thought it could be something special. Dad wants so much to talk to you."

Karen moved away from him and went into the bedroom. She felt like a Ping-Pong ball that was being batted about with no sense of direction.

Cliff followed her. "We can work something out."

"I'm not going to change my plans," Karen said stubbornly.

"Okay, okay," Cliff said, in an attempt to be patient. "Let's see if Dad and I can't change our plans to fit yours. How about going to dinner with us, and then we'll take you to your drama club meeting?"

"What about Mother?" Karen asked. "How do you think she will feel about having you leave the house without visiting with her?"

"You let me handle Mother," Cliff said. "Will you do as I suggest?"

Karen hesitated. "I'll have to check with the fellow who is supposed to come by and pick me up for the meeting."

"It's as good as done then. You call him while I shave. Then you can have the bathroom to get slicked up. Wear that pink suit you had on at The Invite, will you? You looked great in that." Then he added, "Gary thought so, too."

Karen looked suspiciously at Cliff. She didn't know whether he was trying to maneuver her into a good humor or not.

LATER, at dinner, Karen's dad turned to his big news. "I suppose Cliff told you I've been up in the northern part of the state all week?"

Karen nodded. She couldn't speak with her mouth full of spaghetti.

"I've located a piece of property that I'm going to buy. It's about thirty acres now, with promise of more if I wish to purchase it at a later date. There is a small *A*-frame house on a hill overlooking the most beautiful little lake you ever saw."

Karen couldn't quite comprehend what he was saying.

"I'm going to stock the lake with trout. Eventually, I hope to put up a few summer cabins to rent in season."

"Do you mean you're going to live up there, or just use it for vacation?"

"No, it won't be any vacation, Karen. It will be a lot of hard work. Most of the land is in evergreens. I'm going to raise Christmas trees on the property."

"Christmas trees?" she said in disbelief. Somehow she'd never given much thought to anyone actually raising them as a business. "But what about your real estate office?"

"I've sold it. Think how wonderful this can be for us, Karen. You can come and spend your vacations with me there. Cliff is going to work up there this summer. It's something I've always wanted to do."

Her dad did love the out-of-doors, but it had been years since he'd been able to get away from the demands of his business to go fishing or camp out. She remembered that a couple of times, when she was a very small girl, he had taken her up to the mountains. It had been a great adventure then, sleeping in a tent and cooking their meals over an open fire. It might be nice, at that. Better than staying in the apartment all summer with nothing to do while Mother was at work.

"Dad, it sounds great," she agreed.

He gave a sigh of relief. "I'm glad you like the idea."

Then Karen felt that Dad suddenly became ill at ease. She knew he had something else to tell her.

"Karen," he began hesitantly.

He seemed to be looking to Cliff for help, but Cliff appeared as unable as Dad was to speak.

"I've got more news," he said, finally. "I hope you'll be as happy about it as I am."

Karen stared at him dumbly, wondering what could cause him to act this way.

"Karen," he began again, then said abruptly, "I'm going to be married in a couple of weeks."

Once the news was out, both Dad and Cliff talked rapidly.

"You remember Clara Allison," Cliff said. "You met her up at Northwood, at the dance."

Karen was stunned. Her mind conjured up a picture of the tall woman with the large nose and unattractively short-cropped hair.

"We're going to be married in the chapel at Northwood. Clara has worked at the college for about six years, and all her friends are up there. It won't be a large wedding. Cliff is going to stand up with me. Clara wants very much for you to be a junior bridesmaid. She thinks the new blue formal you have will be just right. In fact, she's planned her whole color scheme around it."

Karen's stomach turned over with revulsion as she pictured the grotesque event. Karen knew her lips were trying to form words but no sound was coming out. How could Dad ask such a thing of her?

"You're going to like Clara very much when you get to know her. She's a very fine person and she wants. . . ."

"I don't see how I can possibly come up for the wedding," Karen interrupted. "Things at school are so busy during the last few weeks of school." She knew it sounded exactly like what it was, a weak excuse.

"Karen," Dad was looking at her now, intently seeking out her eyes. "This means a lot to me, to all of us. Clara and I want you to be a participant in the wedding because . . . because we realize that Clara is not just marrying me. It's not that simple. She knows she's marrying into a ready-made family. She's even prepared a special part in the wedding service in which she will pledge herself to accept the responsibility of being my partner in helping to be your parents."

Karen wanted to lash out at that. She hadn't asked Clara to be one of her parents. Why did this woman think she had any right to assume Karen would accept her? She couldn't become Karen's parent if Karen didn't want her.

Karen stood up shakily and said, "It's time for me to go. I've got to be at my meeting."

Cliff reached out and grabbed her arm. "You've got time to be polite and give Dad an answer. After all, he and Clara were nice enough to include you in their plans."

That did it! Karen started to snap, "Thanks, but I don't want to be included," but she looked at her dad. He looked so vulnerable, sitting there waiting for an answer, that she couldn't hurt him. No matter how he had hurt her, she couldn't do it.

Dad said, "Cliff, please. Karen has to make up her own mind about this. Come on, Karen. If you're ready to leave I'll drive you to your meeting now."

They rode in an unpleasant silence to the Community Center. Karen didn't feel at all like attending the drama club meeting, but it was the only excuse she had for escaping from Dad and Cliff and their talk of the wedding.

When she got out of the car, Dad walked with her to the building.

"Please don't make a hasty decision," Dad requested. "Think it over carefully. I'm going to move my things up north next weekend, so be sure to let me know before that time. When you call, we'll make all the arrangements for your trip north."

Karen went inside the Community building. She watched through the glass doors as Dad got into the car and drove away. Then the tears came. She could imagine what Cliff and Dad were talking about. Dad had said her participation in the wedding would be her decision. Her decision! That was a laugh. He was so certain she'd come around to his way of thinking that he had said he would arrange transportation for her when she called him. He didn't even seem to realize how incongruous that was.

Karen searched through her purse for a handkerchief. As she tried to stop the tears and muffle the sounds of her sadness, two boys entered the building. They glanced curiously at her as they walked past. She dodged into the girls' rest room to get away from their stares. She looked into the mirror. Her eyes were puffy and red. She couldn't attend the meeting of the drama club this way.

Karen went outside the building and looked for a bus stop. She walked to the corner. It was getting dark and she felt nervous. The neighborhood was unfamiliar and the streetlight didn't seem like much protection. She'd give anything to be safe at home now.

As Karen waited, a car drew up to the curb beside her. She turned and looked the other direction, hoping that if she ignored him, the driver would leave her alone. She had almost decided to head back for the safety of the Community Center when she heard a voice call to her from the car.

"Karen? Karen Beal?"

Cautiously she turned toward the man in the car, but in the dim light she couldn't make out his features.

"It's Ray Harrison," he said. "I thought it was you standing here on the corner, but I wasn't sure. Did you have any trouble locating the Community building?"

A flood of relief washed over Karen as she recognized Mr. Harrison's voice.

"Get in," he said. "I'll drive around to the parking lot behind the building. There's a ramp at the back door where I usually go inside. Have you been waiting on the corner long?"

"No, only a little while," Karen said.

As Mr. Harrison parked the car in the back lot, Karen remembered her red eyes. "I was really waiting for a bus to go home. I can't stay for the meeting tonight. I've got to go home."

"Is something wrong, Karen?" he asked.

"I'm . . . I'm not feeling very well," she alibied.

"I'll be glad to drive you home," he said, starting the car's motor once more. "I wouldn't want you going on the bus if you're ill."

"Oh, no," she protested. "I can't let you take me home. It's almost time for you to start the meeting."

"The kids will understand."

"Wait," she said. Inexplicably, she found herself telling him the truth. "I'm not really ill. I've been crying, and my eyes are all red. I'm embarrassed for anyone to see me this way."

He didn't look at her. He sat quietly for a moment and then said, "I've got an idea, if you're game to try."

"What is it?" she asked, experimentally.

"I think it's about time our drama club had another lesson in makeup." He looked at his watch. "We've got time before the meeting starts to get you all fixed up as our first demonstration. How about it? I think I can guarantee that not a tear nor a red nose will show."

Karen was glad that she had gone to the drama club meeting that evening. Even though she had been reticent, at first, about meeting a group of strangers, she quickly found herself feeling very much a part of the group. She knew this was due to Ray. All the kids called him Ray, and she found herself doing the same.

Ray did such a skillful job of making her up that she had forgotten completely about her tear-swollen eyes. After teaching them how to apply the various bases, he let them experiment, and they had spent most of the evening working out new effects. One boy did a hilarious job with some actor's putty and created a Cyrano-de-Bergerac nose. He located, in the costume closet, an old sword and a hat with an outrageously long red plume. They all laughed until their stomach muscles ached.

When Ray drove Karen home that evening, he said, "I'll see you next Friday evening. Call me if you need transportation." Then he added, "Call me any time you need me."

Later, as Karen creamed the makeup off her face, she hoped that she could count on Cliff to be his usual lazy self on Saturday morning. If he slept late enough, she could get all her work done and be out of the house before he got up to badger her about being in the wedding. Perhaps if she worked it right, she could manage to stay at Jennie's house until late Sunday evening. That way Cliff would have to leave for Northwood before she got home.

THROUGHOUT the next week, the decision Karen had to make about going to the wedding hung like a fog in her brain. It seemed to darken and infect everything she did or thought.

"Karen, why are you so silent?" Mother would ask. "You're so restless at night, and you haven't been eating well at all. Is everything all right at school?"

Karen would nod, knowing full well that everything wasn't going well at school. She couldn't seem to concentrate on her studies. Her English teacher had called her in for a conference about why she received so poor a grade on the last test. Karen knew her teacher was only trying to help, but Karen just couldn't respond.

She had to admit that Marty's criticism of her work on the paper wasn't just his usual sarcasm. Karen hadn't been doing much more than going through the motions of turning out the feature page lately. It wasn't that she didn't care about the *Town Crier,* but writing feature stories somehow seemed unimportant in comparison to her recent problems.

To make matters worse, Karen had received a letter from Gary on Wednesday. She had opened it so hopefully, thinking it might cheer her up, but she was angered and shocked at what it said:

> Dear Karen:
>
> I was talking to Cliff Sunday night, and he said you will be coming up to Northwood for the wedding in two weeks. He knew I would want to see you. I've been trying to figure out a way that we could spend some time together. I'd like to be able to attend the wedding with you on Saturday afternoon. The only difficulty is that I have signed up to go on a biology class field trip over that weekend.
>
> I think I can manage to come back to campus

late Saturday evening. Cliff said he would drive out to the camp grounds and bring me back to school. We could at least spend Sunday together.

It will be good to see you, since it looks as if I may not be home much during vacation. I have applied for a job as assistant here for the summer. Being an assistant is not as important as it sounds, as I'll be sort of a glorified errand boy and have charge of taking care of the lab animals.

I've got to run now as I'm almost late for class, but I did want to get this in the mail right away to let you know that I'm glad you're coming up here soon.

As ever,
Gary.

Karen crumpled the letter up in her hand. So now Gary knew about the wedding plans! How could Cliff have had the nerve to tell him? Karen knew the answer to that even before she asked it. This was one of Cliff's clever schemes to get her to agree to attend the wedding.

Karen had never been so desperate. She had to talk to someone. She couldn't continue to hold all this confusion inside herself. Mentally she went over the list of persons to whom she might turn for some advice, but no one seemed to present a reasonable possibility. She certainly couldn't talk to her mother. How could she discuss with Mother Dad's approaching marriage to another woman?

Karen couldn't talk to Grandmother. Grandmother's reaction to the divorce was one of stern disapproval. Karen hated to think what a remarriage would evoke.

She might have talked to Jennie about it, but now that Cliff had seen fit to include Gary in the situation, everything had changed. Besides, how could Jennie really understand such a mess, when her own parents got along so well?

She was in Spanish class on Thursday afternoon when it occurred to her who might be able to help. As soon as class was out she hurried to the school office to use the telephone. She looked through the directory and quickly dialed the number. As she listened to the ringing at the other end of the line, she began to fear she had done something foolish. What would he think of her for calling? She really didn't know him very well, but he had said, "Call me any time."

A voice answered, "Station WXMW. What may I do for you?"

Karen took a deep breath and said, "I'd like to speak to Mr. Harrison, please."

"Hold on a minute. I think he's just finishing a telecast."

The bell for last class rang as she waited. Karen started to hang up. Then she heard his voice on the line and she knew she'd done the right thing.

"Hello, Mr. Harrison . . . Ray," she said. "This is Karen Beal and I need to talk to you."

"Certainly, Karen," he said, as though there were nothing unusual in her request. "Do you want to see me right now?"

"I'm still in school. I've got one more class, but I can be at the station by four o'clock."

"I'll pick you up right after school is out. That will save you a bus ride."

Karen felt better already. "Thanks," she said. "Thanks so much. I'll wait for you at the main entrance."

That afternoon as Karen got into Ray's car, she was aware of the fellows and girls staring at her. She wondered how many of them recognized the handsome young man at the wheel as the announcer on "Platter Party."

"I feel kind of silly about calling you," Karen admitted

as the car moved into traffic, "but I just had to talk to someone, and you were the only one I could think of who might
be able to help me."

"I'm glad you called," he said. "Do you mind if we go
to a drive-in and talk while we have a malt? I was too busy
for lunch today."

Karen suspected that the malt was as much for her benefit as for his, and she was grateful for his thoughtfulness.

While they waited for their order, Karen tried to think
of the best way to begin. Ray didn't rush her, he seemed
to be aware of how difficult it was for her to talk about
her problem.

"You know that I was crying when I came to the drama
club meeting the other evening," Karen began.

"I wondered if that was why you called."

"It's a long and involved story," she said. "I'm not sure
I can even make sense out of it now."

"Take your time," he said. "I'm not due back at the studio
until nine this evening."

Once the way was cleared, Karen began telling Ray about
her parents' constant arguing, the divorce, Mother's illness,
and the approaching marriage between her dad and Clara.

"So, I have to call my dad and give him my decision about
whether or not I'll go to the wedding," Karen said.

"And you want to make certain you do the right thing
where everyone is concerned," Ray added.

Karen nodded. "But that doesn't seem possible. Somebody always seems to get hurt these days."

"How do you feel about your dad getting married
again?"

"It seems like a crazy dream. I can't quite believe it.
What if Dad makes another mistake? It seems strange to
think of him falling in love. He's in his forties."

149

"You mean that love is limited only to teen-agers?"

"No, of course not," she said, a bit indignantly.

Ray didn't say anything.

"Yes, I guess what you said is right," she admitted. "I really never thought of it that way before. I suppose older people can fall in love, but it seems so awful when it's your own dad."

"It's hard for you to see the hearts-and-flowers angle?" he asked. "Tell me, how do you feel about the woman your dad is planning to marry?"

"Clara?" she mused. "I don't like her. She's . . . well, I can't imagine anyone wanting to marry her. She's very different from my mother."

"How well do you know her?"

"I met her only once," Karen said.

"Then you don't really know her as a person . . . a human being?"

"No, I suppose not," Karen replied, "but she can't be much if she hasn't gotten married by now. She's at least thirty. She's not at all pretty."

"Now, are you saying that love is only for the attractive persons in this world?"

Karen felt ashamed that she had snared herself in the same narrow trap.

"Why is it?" she cried. "Why is it that I'm always wrong? I don't mean to be this way."

"You're not a villain, Karen," he said. "All of us get caught in circumstances that turn us inside out. Sometimes there really is no right or wrong answer. Sometimes it's a case of having to choose between two unpleasant solutions. The important thing about making a choice is to think carefully about our motives. That's all I was trying to get you to understand, Karen."

"I wish I could get terribly, terribly ill," Karen said. "Then no one could blame me for not going to the wedding."

"Does that mean it's not so much a decision about whether or not to go to the wedding, but how to refuse without hurting your father, your father's bride, or yourself?"

"When you put it that way, I guess that's what I want," Karen said slowly. "I wanted to tell him that I couldn't bear to come to the wedding when he asked me the other night, but he and Cliff ganged up on me. It seems that everybody—Dad, Mother, Cliff—wants me to do exactly as he says. They each pretend to offer me a choice, but they don't, really. If I don't do what one of them wants, I feel selfish and spoiled."

"So, it appears as though someone is going to be hurt, either your father or yourself."

"I guess I've got to be the sacrifice because they're all adults," Karen said angrily. "I've got to be little goody-two-shoes and go to the wedding and behave myself as an obedient daughter should."

"And if you go with that attitude?"

"Then I would still probably wind up hurting somebody," she said, almost crying in her frustration. "Why does life have to be so complicated?"

Ray shook his head and sighed. "You sound very much the way I sounded a few years ago. The only answer I've been able to come up with is that life is complicated because we human beings all have our own problems and needs and hopes, and sometimes we get in each other's way. Sometimes our goals conflict instead of running parallel with one another."

"But what can I do?" Karen pleaded. "Tell me what you'd do if you were in my place."

"Why not try being completely honest with yourself and with your dad. It might hurt, but it will be less involved and less painful in the long run. I don't know if I've really been of any help to you. The burden of the final decision is going to have to rest on you alone."

They sat for a while finishing their malts. Then, Karen said, "There is one more thing." She reached into her purse and took out Gary's letter.

After Ray had read the letter, Karen said, "My brother, Cliff, engineered that little project. It was one of his not-so-subtle attempts to pressure me into saying that I'd go up north. I didn't intend that Gary know about the wedding. It's been bad enough having him know of the trouble at home."

Karen told Ray what had happened Christmas Day, when Gary had seen her dad leaving the house with his suitcase, and how she had later run into him at the drugstore during Mother's illness.

"I've always liked Gary, but I didn't think he was aware that I existed. He never paid particular attention to any of the girls at school. That's why I was so surprised when he invited me up to Northwood for The Invite. I've tried not to push myself at him."

"From the sound of this letter, he thinks a lot of you," Ray said.

"Cliff may have put an end to all that. I'm so embarrassed I can hardly stand it. I don't think I can ever face Gary after this. I thought about writing to Gary and telling him that I never want to see him again."

"I wouldn't cross him off the list so soon," Ray suggested. "From what you've told me, Gary is a very special kind of young man. Why don't you give him credit for some human understanding? If this had bothered him, I doubt if he would have written to you at all."

"He comes from such a wonderful family. I feel so ashamed about my parents' being divorced. I keep thinking there must be something terribly wrong with us. You can't imagine how humiliated I was at the dance when I saw my dad there with Clara. I couldn't explain a thing like that to Gary. All I could do was clam up. Gary thought it was his fault that I acted the way I did."

"Often when we're hurt or angry, we lash out at the wrong target. Why don't you tell Gary why you've been so upset lately? It's better than letting him misinterpret your actions. If he means anything at all to you, why not trust him by being honest with him? If he's the right kind of fellow, he'll understand."

"Thanks so much, Ray. You're the first person that I've been able to talk to honestly for a long time."

"If you ever need to talk again, don't hesitate to call me, any time."

"I feel as if I've imposed on you enough already," she said.

"Karen," he answered her, earnestly. "Friends don't consider it an imposition. I know what it means to have friends who are willing to help. I figure the best method for me to repay people's interest in me is to be ready if ever I can help someone else."

When Karen went upstairs, her mother was anxiously waiting for her.

"Karen," she exclaimed, "I've been nearly out of my mind worrying. I've called everyone I could think of, and no one knew where you were. Do you have any idea what time it is?"

153

"I'm sorry, Mother," Karen said. "I thought I'd be home before you got here. I was with Ray Harrison."

"Do you mean that crippled man from the television station?"

"He's not as crippled as you think," Karen replied.

"What do you mean by that?"

"I mean he's got a lot healthier attitude about life than most of us have. I had to talk to somebody who could give me some good advice. Ray was nice enough to listen to me for most of the afternoon."

Mother started to say something and then checked herself. "Let's eat," she said, instead, "before everything is stone cold."

After dinner, as Karen was drying dishes, the doorbell rang. Mother answered it.

"Karen, you're wanted on the phone downstairs," she called.

As Karen stepped out into the hallway, her mother said, "I don't want you and Jennie to stay on the phone longer than five minutes."

Karen walked past the glowering apartment manager.

"It's not your gabby girl friend, this time," he informed her. "It's a man."

Karen picked up the receiver, aware that the manager was pretending to be busy in the lobby so that he could stay near while she was on the phone. He acted as though he rented it by the hour.

"Hello," she said. "This is Karen Beal."

"Hello, baby," said her dad. "I've been waiting all week for you to call."

"Well, I. . . ." Karen couldn't seem to control her voice. "I've been busy, Dad." She emphasized the word *Dad* for the manager's enlightenment. Let him make something out of that.

"Karen, we need to talk about your trip north."

Karen's mind sorted out every excuse she could think of. She could plead too much homework or some school activity, but she was haunted by what Ray had said.

"Dad, I'm not coming," she said simply.

There was a silence on the other end of the line. At first she thought he had hung up.

At last he said, "We really want you there, both Clara and I."

"I know you do, Dad," Karen said, not wanting to cry. "I'd come if I could, but I just can't do it. I don't think I'd fit in."

"Did your mother have anything to do with your decision?"

"Oh, no," Karen replied, surprised that he should ask such a question. "No, of course not. I didn't even discuss it with her. I don't know if she's heard the news or not. Cliff might have mentioned it. You'll have to ask him."

Karen knew he was intensely disappointed. She felt terrible. She hated herself for not being able to do as he wanted. She hated the manager of the apartment for standing there listening to her conversation, and not even caring about the pain people caused each other. She tried not to hate Cliff and Clara and her dad for forcing her into such a position.

Limply she said, "Dad, I have to go now."

She hung up and turned to the manager, who stood staring at her. She returned his stare with all the animosity she could muster.

Then she walked slowly and deliberately to the service stairs and started up to the apartment. Halfway up, she sat on the steps and leaned against the railing . . . and cried.

11.

Strange New Summer

SEVERAL things led to Karen's decision to spend part of the summer up north with her dad and Clara. As usual, Karen felt swept along with the tide. She knew she wasn't choosing what to do so much as she was reacting to other things which had happened.

Mother hadn't felt well one day in late May. She had stayed away from work. Karen came home from school that afternoon to find her mother sitting in the small occasional chair in the bedroom. When Karen came into the room, she sensed something was wrong. She glanced about the room and noticed the open suitcase with the blue formal Dad had bought her spread out across it.

"Where did this dress come from?" Mother asked in a strident voice that was reminiscent of the bitter days before the divorce.

Karen was overwhelmed with a desire to escape the painful confrontation. She was tempted to say, "It's one of Jennie's," but she had never been able to lie to her mother before and she wasn't able to do so now.

Karen said, "It's mine."

"I assumed it was yours, but where did it come from?"

Karen faced her mother defiantly. "Dad bought it for me when I went up to Northwood for The Invite."

With false bravado Karen dug into the suitcase for the slim jims and blouse. She threw them on the bed nonchalantly.

"He bought these for me, too," she said.

"Karen, I simply cannot understand how you could have been so devious."

Karen felt anger flame up in her. "Maybe you forced me to hide them. I didn't tell you because you always get so upset whenever his name is metioned. I was trying to avoid a scene."

"But, Karen, I bought you a beautiful new suit for the trip. I cannot imagine why you would go to your father to ask for these other things."

"I didn't see any reason why I shouldn't ask my own dad to buy me a new dress. You said we didn't have any money for new clothes. I didn't know you were going to surprise me with the suit."

Mother appeared to be at a loss for an answer. Karen hoped this would end the conversation. At least the clothing was out in the open now, and she could wear it. She turned to leave the room.

"Don't go, Karen. I still have something to say to you."

Karen returned obediently and braced herself.

"I thought you understood that we were going to get along without your father's help. We don't want to be obligated to him."

Karen was so bewildered at her mother's distorted reasoning, she could hardly speak. "That was your idea. I didn't agree to that. I don't even understand it. After all, it's not my divorce."

Mother stood and started toward her.

"Don't you ever talk to me like that again, young lady. I endured twenty years of marriage for your sake. I tried my best not to resort to divorce, but your father. . . ."

Mother waited for a moment and then said in a determinedly regulated voice, "We can get along without your father. He does not want the responsibility of caring for this family. He never did. I'm happy to relieve him of that. It ought to be obvious to you by now that he has chosen a new life for himself. I think it would be wise for us to do the same."

The incident which convinced Karen she needed to get away occurred during the next to last week of school.

Karen was hard at work preparing two special insert pages for the *Town Crier,* featuring stories about the graduating seniors. Marty Riffner came over and sat down at the table near her. For once, Karen did not stiffen for the expected sarcasm. Marty had mellowed appreciably since the First Class trophy for division "A" school papers resided in the glass case in the hall, with his name as editor engraved on it.

Marty sorted through the cuts for which she was writing captions.

"What are you doing?" she asked. "Did you come to check on whether I'm writing you up properly as the winner of the Elliott Memorial Journalism Scholarship?"

Surprisingly, Marty had no bright remark. He seemed unusually subdued.

"What do you plan to be doing this summer?" Marty asked.

"After I get back from the journalism workshop, I may try to get a job. A friend of my mother's thinks there might be an opening in the *Dispatch* business office."

"That's good," Marty said. "It will give you something to do this summer. I guess you'll be kind of lonely with Gary staying up at Northwood."

What was Marty getting at? Karen wasn't about to say anything that he could report to Gary.

"I haven't any claims on Gary," she said, defensively.

"Are you planning to go to the *Town Crier* banquet?"

"Well, of course. I've never missed one yet, besides. . . ." Karen had been about to say that she wouldn't miss that banquet for anything in the world. Next year's staff would be announced that evening. It would be her big night.

Marty shifted in his chair uncomfortably.

"Listen, Marty, I'm ahead of deadline now, but if you sit here talking I'm going to be scrounging at the last minute," Karen said.

"I wanted to tell you something," he said. He leaned close to her and said in a confidential voice, "I'm not supposed to tell you this, but I accidentally saw the list of next year's staff appointments on Miss Gray's desk. I didn't mean to look, but I couldn't help it."

Karen's heart pounded with anticipation. Why was Marty telling her this?

"Karen, I didn't want you to go to the banquet and find out there but . . ." he paused. "Karen, you're not going to be editor of the *Town Crier* next year."

Karen was stunned, first with disbelief, and then indignation.

"Marty Riffner!" she said irately. "You and your practical jokes! I don't think that was amusing at all. You ought to have better sense."

"I wasn't joking. Not about something like that," he said quietly.

"Marty, you've delighted in saying some pretty hateful

things to me. Well, I hope you enjoyed this to the fullest. You can go and have your little laugh now."

"I wasn't trying to hurt you or laugh at you, Karen. I thought maybe it would be easier for you to accept if you found out now, and it didn't have to come as a complete surprise at the banquet."

When she met Jennie at the locker after school that afternoon, Karen's disappointment had been transformed into reproach for Marty. Jennie listened as Karen vented her anger.

"I've always thought Marty Riffner was hateful, but how could he stoop that low?"

"Are you sure, absolutely sure that Marty wanted to hurt you?"

"Why else? You know how Marty has always felt about me." Karen stacked her books on top of the pile in the locker.

"Yes, I know," Jennie said, slowly and purposefully, "I know exactly how Marty has always felt about you. I should have been half so lucky to have him feel that way about me."

Karen whirled and faced Jennie. "What does that mean?"

"It means that Marty has always liked you."

"He's got a strange way of showing it," Karen said, skeptically.

"I guess he was reacting to the fact that he knew he didn't have a chance with you."

Karen was flippantly casual that evening when she revealed the news at home. Mr. Forrester had invited Karen and her mother to his apartment for a delicatessen meal of submarine sandwiches and chili.

"It looks as though you're going to save some money on

me this summer, Mother," she said. "I won't be going to the journalism workshop after all."

In response to her mother's puzzled look, Karen explained, "I found out today that I'm not going to be editor of the paper next year."

She knew her mother was at a loss for words. She also knew that Mother was trying not to show how disappointed she was, how her mother hurt for her. "It may be for the best, Karen. I've had the feeling that you tend to take on too many activities. I didn't really see how you were going to manage to handle the extra duties on the paper."

"Let's face it," Karen said caustically. "I couldn't handle it. Miss Gray knew that when she chose someone else."

"Karen, this might be the opportune time for you to reconsider transferring to Central High. There's really nothing to keep you at Marshall next year. You'll admit it has been a difficult time for you."

"I'll admit that all right," Karen said.

"Why don't you make the change? It would give you a rest."

"That would be running away, wouldn't it?" Karen asked. "But, I am going to take a rest. I'm going to spend the summer up at Dad's ranch."

"I think we'd better talk about this later," Mother said, sharply.

Later, when Karen told Ray that she was planning to go up north to spend the summer with her dad and Clara, he seemed pleased.

"This could be a wonderful chance for you to get to know Clara," he said, "and perhaps you'll get to know your dad all over again. Give them both a chance. Remember, we're all in this human predicament together."

MOTHER didn't want Karen to go north for the summer. Karen was convinced that it wasn't just that she didn't want Karen to be away; she didn't want her to be with Dad. However, Karen was persistent, and during the third week in June she was on her way north.

When Karen got off the train, she saw the tall, angular figure of her stepmother waiting for her on the platform. Clara was wearing beige twill western riding trousers and matching beige sweaters. Her sun-bleached hair was cropped in a severely mannish cut with only the hint of a wave at the temples. She wore no makeup. As she came closer she smiled. Karen noticed that she did have even white teeth and though she wasn't at all pretty, she seemed pleasant enough.

Karen thought of what Ray had said, "Try to meet her as a new friend. Don't form any opinions about her in your mind ahead of time. Give her a chance."

Karen took a determined breath. She was going to try.

"How good it is to have you here," Clara said.

Karen didn't really know what to call her. Mother had always frowned on calling adults by their first names, so she couldn't refer to her as Clara. Karen couldn't call her Miss Allison, because she wasn't that anymore. And Karen would have felt like an idiot calling her Mrs. Beal. The last thing in her mind that she could have called her was impossible. She couldn't say *Mother*. To solve the dilemma, Karen tried to avoid the necessity of using any direct term of address.

"Hello," Karen said self-consciously, wondering where Cliff and Dad were.

Clara seemed to be aware of her anxiety.

"Something unexpected came up at the ranch. Your dad and Cliff couldn't come. They wanted to," she assured

Karen, "but you'll see what detained them when we get home."

As they rode along, Karen was aware that they were climbing higher into the rolling foothills. Karen looked through her purse for a scarf to keep the wind from blowing her long hair and tangling it beyond repair, but she didn't have one. She tried in vain to hold her hair in place with both hands. She couldn't help but notice that Clara's short hair was hardly disturbed at all. It wasn't particularly stylish, but it was cerainly neat and practical.

"Isn't it beautiful up here?" Clara continued to chat. "It's a grand climate, too."

In a way, Karen was glad that Clara kept the conversation going. It tended to ease their strangeness with each other.

"I guess Dad really likes this life," Karen said.

"Doesn't he though!" Clara said enthusiastically. "This is what he has always dreamed about. When he got the chance to trade for this land he was just like a little kid with a new toy. Wait until you see him, you'll know what I mean. He's a different person."

The house on the hill was different from any Karen had ever been in. "*A*-frame" was the perfect name for it. It did look exactly like a tall *A* perched on the side of the mountain, with its sharply slanted roof. When Karen went inside, she had the feeling she was entering a ski lodge. Not that she had ever been in a ski lodge, but it was like pictures she'd seen. The front and back walls of the *A* were almost completely glassed in, so that the interior of the house was very light, and there was a beautiful view in almost every direction. An oversized stone fireplace dominated the front room. The large beams which supported the second floor looked like gigantic logs.

Clara noticed her interest in them and said, "Those beams are all hand-hewn. The man who owned this place did all the work himself. Don't you think the house is much larger than it appears from the outside? Come on, I'll show you where you'll stay."

Karen looked tentatively inside the room that was to be hers this summer. She had to admit that it was charming. There were blue-and-white-checked café curtains at the windows. The furniture was painted white with blue trim. The bedspread flounces of white eyelet matched the ruffled skirt on the vanity table. There was a blue and white checked coverlet of the same material as the curtains.

"Put your things away, and we'll go down and see what the men are doing."

Karen took her time unpacking. She hadn't even started on her second suitcase when she heard Clara calling her.

"Better get a move on, Karen. We've only got an hour until I must start lunch."

Karen dressed in the orange slim jims and blouse that Dad had bought her. She brushed her hair back and tied it into a secure ponytail to protect it from the wind which seemed to blow continuously up here on the hill.

When Karen went downstairs, she saw that Clara was dusting and straightening a stack of magazines on a low sleek table.

"Do you like Danish modern furniture?" Clara asked. "I spent a year in Europe and grew to appreciate its clean functional lines while I was in Scandinavia. I started collecting pieces when I went to work at Northwood. I had all this jammed into a tiny apartment. I was so thrilled with this house because it seemed to be made to order."

Karen nodded and couldn't help thinking that a single girl probably had plenty of money to go to Europe and to

164

buy furniture. She wondered what Dad thought about it. She couldn't quite imagine him in this setting.

Clara started out the door, then stopped and said, "You'd better put on a sweater, Karen. The sun looks warm, but there is a cool breeze."

Karen said, "We'll only be outside for a while. You said we didn't have much time. I'll be okay."

"Please get a sweater," Clara said, rather stiffly. "I'm not going to have you become ill while you're here in my care."

Karen felt every muscle in her body tense up. For a moment she contemplated saying, "I'm a big girl now, I can take care of myself," but she turned and went upstairs for a sweater without speaking.

Karen followed Clara along a path around the back of the house and through a stand of scrub cedar.

"There," Clara said, and pointed to the West. "Can you see it?"

Karen squinted, and through the trees on the next rise of ground she saw what appeared to be a shed with a fenced-in area. There were moving forms. Clara started to run.

When they approached the shed, Karen realized that what she saw was a corral with horses. There were three, no . . . four. Palominos. And there was Dad.

Dad hurried toward her and grabbed her and swung her around as he used to do when she was little.

"What do you think about all this?" he asked, taking in the ranch with a sweeping movement of his hand. "The horses should have been delivered yesterday, but we got a call they would be here this morning. Cliff and I thought it would be best for us to stay here and get them all unloaded and accustomed to their new surroundings. Aren't they beauties?"

Karen grinned as she observed her dad's pride in his new possessions.

He turned back to her. "Let me look at you. You're taller, aren't you?"

"No," she said. "I've lost some weight. Maybe that makes me seem taller." She looked at Dad. "You're looking pretty good yourself. You're so tan."

"That's what being in the out-of-doors does for me."

"Where's Cliff?" Karen asked, rather reluctantly. She wasn't sure how he would react to her, since she hadn't come to the wedding. Strange that she should feel apologetic toward Cliff. He was the one who had behaved with such inexcusably bad taste by involving Gary.

"Cliff is in the shed working on one of the stalls. Goldie was a bit skittish and did a little damage when he gave her a tour of her new home."

Cliff emerged from the shed. Karen saw that he was even more browned from the sun than Dad.

"Hi, Sis," he said warily.

Karen suspected that he felt the same uncertainty that she did.

"Well, don't I get a kiss from my big brother?" she teased.

A feeling of well-being swept over Karen as Cliff kissed her noisily on the cheek. It was good to clear away the debris of the past months.

Dad put his arm about Karen's shoulder and hugged her to him. "This is going to be the best summer we've ever spent. It's going to be the way I always hoped life would be."

Karen would have like to go back to the corral with Dad

and Cliff, but Clara seemed eager to have her come back and see the kitchen and help with lunch, so Karen went up to the house.

"Can you cook?" Clara asked, as she began to lay out food for lunch.

"As long as it's nothing too elaborate," Karen said. "I enjoy baking."

"There are some boiled potatoes in the refrigerator. How would you like to make the potato salad for lunch? I'll fry some cubed steaks."

Karen felt rather awkward in an unfamiliar kitchen as she hunted for utensils and spices. She managed to get everything assembled and started peeling the soft skins from the potatoes and chopping onions, celery, boiled eggs.

As Karen began to put the dressing into the bowl, Clara said suddenly, "Wait, you're not going to put that on the salad, are you?"

"Yes, what's wrong?"

Clara tasted it and made a wry face. "I think you've got far too much mustard in it. Your dad prefers something more bland."

"This is the way Mother always made it."

"Yes, I know," Clara replied.

Karen felt as though someone had drenched her in hot water. It had never occurred to her that Dad would discuss Mother's cooking with Clara. To find out now that he disliked food he had eaten for years filled Karen with dismay.

"Whatever you wish," Karen said, and moved away, letting Clara take over the mixing of the salad dressing. "I'll set the table."

During lunch, Karen couldn't help watching her dad as he took seconds on the salad.

"This is the best yet," he said to Clara.

"You can thank your daughter for that," she said. "It was her project."

Karen winced. It didn't seem necessary for Clara to be so patently condescending.

"I hope you enjoy the dressing," Karen said. "Clara explained to me how you prefer it without mustard."

For the most part, the summer vacation passed rather uneventfully for Karen. She had a few minor skirmishes with Clara. Karen was somewhat taken aback to have Dad invariably sympathize with Clara instead of with his daughter.

Karen felt that Clara's determination to maintain a rigid schedule and her insistence on rules were confining.

Once she had complained to her dad, "She treats me like a baby."

Dad had replied placatingly, "Remember, Karen, Clara has never had a teen-age daughter before. She's trying to do the right thing. Give her a chance."

Karen tried, honestly tried, not to be irritated at being reminded to brush her teeth and not stay up too late at night, reading. Karen did find it difficult not to be provoked at Clara's apprehension that some of her prized possessions might be damaged by the intrusion of a teen-ager in the house.

Most of the time, Karen managed to avoid unpleasant incidents by staying outside as much as possible. She found that there were innumerable things she could do to help Dad. She enjoyed feeding the horses, and she spent hours currying them.

During the last week of Karen's visit to the ranch, Dad gave her permission to invite Gary to come from Northwood for her birthday celebration. It turned out to be one of the nicest birthdays she had ever had.

Clara drove Karen in to the station in the early morning to meet Gary's train. When they got back to the ranch, Clara insisted that she was going to do everything for the party by herself. Karen was to spend the entire day with Gary.

A whole summer full of Karen's dreams were crowded into that one day which she and Gary had together. Cliff saddled Goldie and Robin for them and they spent the morning riding over the wooded slopes. That afternoon they swam and sunned themselves at the lake. Karen knew it wouldn't have mattered what they did that day, the wonderful part was being together and laughing and talking and feeling that somehow they were part of their own very special world.

Clara insisted that everyone get dressed up for dinner. She had set the table with her best china and crystal. The tall white tapers in the silver candle holders were encircled by tiny pink roses from the garden. Karen had to admit that it couldn't have been nicer. Clara had outdone herself with the dinner. After everyone stuffed himself with roast beef and baked potatoes, Clara went to the kitchen and came back with an elaborately decorated and candle-brightened cake.

Karen took a deep breath and huffed at the cake. In a moment there was nothing but a curling little cloud of smoke from all the extinguished candles.

After Karen had cut the cake, a pile of presents appeared. Clara had bought her a pair of jodhpurs, and her dad added a set of forest-green sweaters. Cliff gave her a box of stationery with her initials engraved in the upper left hand corner of each sheet.

There was a large box from Longman's which had come in the mail from Mother during the week. Inside was a soft gray coat with a ruff of matching fur about the collar. Karen gasped when she saw the label which said it was cashmere.

Dad dulled the sharp edge of her joy a bit when he said, "Your mother always did have extravagant tastes."

There was another package which had come from home in the mail. She had been surprised to note Ray Harrison's return address in the corner. She remembered she had told him in an earlier letter that she had invited Gary out to the ranch for her birthday.

When she unwrapped Ray's present, she discovered it was a book. The protective book jacket pictured a television studio with young people grouped about a table. Ray Harrison was in the center. Karen gave a little squeal as she recognized herself at his left. The title of the book was, "Teens Talk It Over." It was by Ray Harrison. She nearly dropped the book in her excitement to show it around the table.

"Look!" she said, aware that her voice was louder than it should have been. "Ray has written a book about his panel discussions, and I'm on the cover."

They all gathered about the book excitedly. Cliff opened it and said, "There's something written inside."

Karen read it aloud proudly, "To Karen, one of the young people who helped make this book possible."

"I hardly know what to say," Dad remarked. "We've never had a celebrity in the house before."

"Ray's the real celebrity," Karen said, "and he deserves to be."

When the excitement over the book had abated, Karen opened a package from Jennie. It was a set of two tiny golden beetles inset with multicolored rhinestones.

Karen saved Gary's gift for last. The card he gave her was obviously for a child who was just becoming seven, but he had carefully added the numeral 1 in front of the 7. Karen knew immediately why he had selected such a card. When it was opened, a fold-out picture of a merry-go-round emerged. He had written beneath it, "For the girl who deserves to win the gold ring."

She felt a shiver of excitement as she untied the ribbon and removed the paper from his gift. It was a record made by the Northwood choir, called "Serenade."

As Cliff examined the record, he didn't have any of his flippant remarks to tease her with. Karen knew he was involved with his own thoughts. Maybe he was remembering the serenade and thinking of Sally.

After dinner, Clara shooed them all out of the kitchen while she did the dishes.

Karen put the new record on Clara's stereo, turned up the volume, and opened the large sliding windows of the living room so they could hear it as she and Gary sat in the glider swing on the small patio outside.

With the reflection of the moon on the lake below, it was as though the heavens were celebrating her birthday by scattering the water with their own brand of glittering confetti.

Karen rested her head on the back of the glider so that she could look up at the stars embedded in the blue-black sky.

"Somehow I wish we could make time stop right here and now," Karen said. "Everything is so peaceful, and there doesn't seem to be a problem or an unmade decision anywhere."

"But time doesn't stand still, does it?" Gary answered.

"In an hour I've got to be at the station on the train. Back at Northwood there are lab animals to be fed and experiments to be charted. In two weeks classes will start."

"Don't remind me," Karen sighed. "I used to think my senior year in school was going to be glorious, but now I dread it. It's going to be a drag."

"You'll think differently once you've graduated. You'll wonder where the time went."

"If I could just eliminate this year of high school, I wouldn't mind at all."

"Maybe it looks like more of a lark than it actually is," Gary said, "but I do wish you were going to be up at Northwood with me this year."

They sat quietly until Gary turned to her suddenly and said, "There is a way you could get up to Northwood this year—this school year, that is."

"You're kidding," Karen exclaimed. "How?"

"Graduate in mid-term. You've done well in school. I'll bet you've got enough credits."

"I don't know," Karen said, dazed at the prospect. "I never gave it any thought. Maybe I could do it."

From inside the house Karen could hear the record. The choir was singing, "Goodnight, Sweetheart." She knew that Gary heard it, too, for he turned toward her.

"It would be nice not to have to write letters or catch a train when we wanted to see each other."

He kissed her just as the last notes of the music faded away.

The evening was over, but after Karen and Clara had driven home from taking Gary to the station, Karen went back out to the patio. She looked at the lake and then up at the sky. She would like to see the stars from Northwood's observatory with Gary.

12.

The Important Weeks

KAREN's homecoming from the ranch was more exciting than she had imagined it would be. There wasn't a moment for her to slip back into the routine which she and Mother had observed at the end of the school year.

Phil Forrester drove Mother to the train to meet Karen. Before she had time to ask questions, she was whisked home, directed to put on her best clothes and be ready to leave the apartment in half an hour. No one would tell her where they were going.

Mother pressed Karen's pink linen suit while Karen bathed and hunted through her luggage for her good white shoes. Usually Karen hated to have to get ready to go somewhere in such a hurry. She always felt half-dressed, but tonight there was such an air of expectancy she didn't have time to worry about it.

"Mother, have I got time to call Jennie before we leave? I've got to tell her I'm home," Karen said.

"Absolutely not. Phil is going to pick us up in five minutes, and you girls have never talked on the phone less than an hour," Mother said determinedly, but there was nothing harsh in her voice.

Karen could not help noticing that her mother was more radiant than she had been in years.

"Isn't that a new dress?" Karen asked.

"Yes," her mother said, pirouetting so that Karen could see all of the sleek-fitting sheath. "Do you like it? I got it especially for tonight."

Karen had to admit that her mother looked beautiful.

There was a knock on the door, and Phil stuck his head inside.

"Are you two girls ready?"

He was holding his hands behind his back secretively.

"Stand close together," he instructed them. "I want to see how both of you look." He whistled appreciatively. "I'm the luckiest man in town to be taking two such beautiful gals out to dinner."

From behind his back he revealed two large florist boxes.

Karen opened hers and found fragrant white gardenias framed with deep-red rose buds.

"They're lovely," Karen said, "but won't you tell me where we're going?"

"You'll find out," he said, and winked as he helped Mother pin on the largest purple orchid Karen had ever seen.

When they went downstairs, Karen was surprised to find Ray Harrison waiting for them in his car.

"Get in," Ray invited. "I'm the chauffeur for this little shindig tonight."

"Ray," Karen said, "it's great to see you. Maybe you'll tell me what all the mystery is."

"You'll find out," he said, smiling secretively.

Not only did they eat, but they were guests of honor at a banquet held in one of the largest hotels in town. Karen was still confused, but little by little the whole picture began to come into focus, as she saw the information directory in the hotel lobby. It announced the "Art Guild Annual Banquet" in the Terrace Room.

Karen couldn't seem to move her head fast enough to catch sight of all the people who came to greet Phil Forrester.

He would say, "This is Mr. Ellis, head of the Rocky Mountain Association," or "This is Mrs. Vinson, curator of the Vinson Art Gallery."

Karen stopped trying to remember names and faces. She simply shook hands and smiled until her face hurt. She was immeasurably relieved when they were finally allowed to sit down and eat.

Before she had finished her ham and peas, the microphone at the head table was switched on and the master of ceremonies began a long series of introductions and acknowledgments. Karen tried to continue her meal unobtrusively and listen at the same time to the master of ceremonies, who was saying, "Now, the event that we have all been waiting for. I'm most pleased to announce that this year's Fellowship Grant is being awarded to a local artist who has been a long-time member of the Art Guild. We have known him best for his outstanding work in another area, that of newspaper cartoon editorials. Tonight, however, we recognize his accomplishment in the media of oil portraiture. This year's Guild Artist—Phillip Forrester."

Karen looked at her mother as Mr. Forrester made his way through the applauding group to the platform. Mother's face beamed with reflected happiness.

The crowd quieted as Mr. Forrester accepted his award.

"Sometimes a man has a lifetime dream that's never more than that. It comes to nothing if he's content to merely dream and refuses to venture out into the mainstream of life where earnest endeavor is not always rewarded." He paused and looked toward Mother. "Sometimes a man is lucky enough to find a source of courage and inspiration to make his dream become reality." He made a sweeping motion toward the crowd with outspread arms.

The ripple of applause grew to a tumult. One by one, the diners rose at their places to give him a standing ovation.

"Now," said the master of ceremonies, "we will adjourn to the exhibition hall next door, where we have an exceptionally fine display of work by artists throughout this state. Of course you will all want to see the award-winner by Phillip Forrester."

Phil's picture was the most unusually impressive portrait Karen had ever seen. She wasn't sure why it was called a portrait, for it showed two people. Then, Karen realized that the two people were actually one. The left side of the canvas was misted in soft shades of purple and blue. The face which emerged from the hazy color was barely discernible, but it had a sad expression, dominated by tragic eyes. The blue and purple faded into soft rose and pink on the other side. Another face appeared from this hazy dawn-like background. This face glowed with a serene happiness.

The more Karen looked at the portrait, the more certain she was that she knew who the model for the painting was. The expressive eyes were those of her mother—as they had been, and as they were now.

Phil whispered, "I can only take so much of this hand-shaking business. Let's see if we can't make a quiet getaway."

Gradually they moved toward the doorway and were out in the hall and then out of the building getting into Ray's car.

As THEY sat around the kitchen table late that night, eating the last of a pineapple upside-down cake Mother had baked, Karen asked, "What is this fellowship grant? What does it mean?"

"It means that I'm finally going to do something I've dreamed about for years. I'm going to buy a trailer and spend a year in Mexico, painting wherever and whatever I want."

"What about your job with the newspaper?" Karen inquired.

"The *Dispatch* has been very generous to me. They've asked that I continue to contribute to them whenever I wish, but I'll not be on the staff any longer."

"But what will you do after the year is up?"

"I have hopes of being able to live on what I make from selling my paintings by that time. If I can't make it, I can add to my income with a small art studio, possibly on the West Coast. I've always wanted to live by the ocean."

"Phil's fellowship grant means something else," Mother said.

"It means that you can have a trip to Mexico as a graduation present," Phil cut in.

Karen looked at her Mother questioningly.

"It's no joke," Phil said, and took Mother's hand in his own large one. He was grinning broadly like a child who has brought home all A's on his report card. "Your mother and I are going to be married. We want you to go to Mexico with us as soon as school's out."

Mother nodded happily. "You might even consider postponing college for a year. We could all stay down there together."

Karen watched them as they sat across from her at the kitchen table. She knew it hadn't really been any surprise to her that they were going to get married. As she thought back over the past few months, all the signs were there. Mother had been slowly transformed back into the gay person full of the joy of life that she had once been. Karen understood Phil's portrait of her mother. She hoped with all her heart that Mother had finally found what she had been seeking for so long.

"Well, Karen," Mother asked, "what do you think?"

"I think I'm very happy for both of you. Have you set a date yet?"

"Around the first of the year. We've still got a lot of plans to make," Mother said.

"But, we don't have to make them here tonight," Phil added. "Karen has been on the train most of the day. It's been an exciting evening. I think perhaps it's time we all say 'Good night,' and get some rest."

After Karen was in bed and had turned out the lights, and after Mother had stopped chattering like a schoolgirl, Karen lay in the darkness trying to decide what she should do. The trip to Mexico sounded exciting, but she couldn't help remembering how out of place she had been up at the ranch with Dad and Clara. No matter how much they might want to include her, she wasn't a part of their new life together. The more she thought about it, the more she was determined to do one thing, return to Marshall, and as soon as school started in September, to check with her counselor about the possibility of graduating midterm.

GARY had been right, Karen conceded, when he said that someday she'd look back and wonder where her senior year had gone. It all happened so fast. Surprisingly, she did have a few regrets now that it was almost over.

Of course, her senior year went faster than most, because

she was graduating midterm. Now, in the second week of December, she was only one month away from the final day.

Another thing which made the year fly by was the job she had working after school and on Saturdays. Ray Harrison had urged her to accept the position as a helper at the Community Center Day Nursery.

Karen was nervous about it, at first, since she had never been around small children very much, except for Jennie's younger sisters and brother. The longer she worked at the nursery, however, the more she enjoyed it. Sometimes Karen perceived that these children from a blighted area of town were helping her much more than she helped them. She found herself lavishing the love and attention on them that they didn't receive from tired mothers who found it necessary to work all day to keep their families subsisting.

Karen would come home at dinner time exhausted, but content. She had difficulty not repeating to Mother everything each child had said and done throughout the entire afternoon.

Tired as she was, however, there never seemed a moment to relax. Mother and Phil spent almost every evening visiting showrooms and pricing trailers. Karen stayed home and wrote long letters to Gary and worked on her lessons.

Karen couldn't help thinking how different the coming Christmas season was going to be from that of last year. She planned to go up north and spend the first week of the Christmas holiday with Dad and Clara. Then, Dad's letter came.

> Dear Karen:
>
> This is to tell you that it has been necessary to change our plans a bit. We will have to cancel

179

your trip up here at Christmastime. As you probably know, we have started loading our first shipments of Christmas trees. More orders have come in than we had even hoped, but it has increased the work load considerably. We've had to rig up special lights so that we can cut and load late into the night. I've had to hire several high school boys from town to help me. They're inexperienced, so we don't move quite as fast as I would like, but Cliff won't be able to get over here for another week and Clara isn't able to help at all.

Clara's health is another reason we'll have to call off your visit at this time. The doctor tells us that there'll be a new member of the family next May . . . that is, if Clara keeps off her feet. She's had a pretty rough time of it so far, and I've been very worried about her.

We'll look forward to seeing you another time, perhaps next summer.

Love,
Dad

Karen didn't know why she should be surprised at anything any more, but somehow she couldn't quite picture Clara and Dad as the parents of a new baby. She felt as though this almost closed the door between them now. What did it matter? She didn't really need any of them, she thought defiantly. She'd soon be at Northwood, and no one would have to worry about what to do with her.

In spite of her bravado, Karen couldn't help being hurt that Dad didn't come to graduation. Even though Clara might not have been up to making the trip, Dad could have come himself or sent a card or given some indication that he was thinking about her on this occasion.

Gary drove down that evening with Cliff and Sally. Ray Harrison met them all at the restaurant where Phil had arranged a dinner party in Karen's honor. Grandmother Newsome had arrived a few days before and was planning to stay on for a week while Mother and Phil were on their wedding trip.

"In a way," Mother said, cheerily, "I'm glad you decided to graduate midterm. There'll be less confusion at the ceremony. I remember how weary I was when Cliff graduated."

"I remember that we had the commencement service in the football stadium," said Cliff. "We sat on bleachers, and they were terribly uncomfortable. I couldn't locate you in that crowd.

"I guess I wasn't a particularly outstanding student," Cliff said, "not like Karen, at any rate."

"I'm glad we're going to get to sit inside the auditorium and we'll be able to see her and hear her when she gives the farewell response on behalf of the graduates," Mother said, proudly.

"I hope I don't forget my speech and disgrace us all," Karen said, referring to the farewell response she was to make.

After they had eaten and Karen had opened several gifts, they drove to the auditorium at Marshall High.

As they parked the cars and gathered to go into the building together, Ray commented that Karen was probably the graduate with the largest personal rooting section.

Karen left them at the entrance and went backstage to put her robe on. One of the boys backstage discovered a tiny hole in the heavy velvet stage curtains and was peeking

181

out through it at the crowded auditorium. He was describing, in hilarious terms and with vigorous gestures, the hats worn by several women in the audience.

In a few moments, Karen heard the first notes of "Pomp and Circumstance." She waited restlessly for her turn to begin the march across the stage.

Karen sat motionless, with a glassy-eyed pretense of attention. The superintendent of schools was announced, and he launched into a laborious introduction of awards.

"Not only has this student exhibited scholastic excellence by maintaining a high grade point average over most of the four years of matriculation. . . ."

Karen had to force herself to listen to what the man was saying as her eyes traveled up and down the rows of parents seated in the auditorium before her. She had no trouble locating Gary, Mother, Phil, and the others, but why couldn't she find her dad?

The superintendent continued, "This student has also shown leadership qualities by participating in various extra-curricular activities at the school. Furthermore there has been demonstrated a concern for the welfare of others through her work with children at the Community Center. Now, in recognition of her competence and potential of future accomplishment, the Society of American Dames has awarded their Achievement Scholarship worth two hundred and fifty dollars to Karen Beal."

Karen heard her name and was vaguely aware of being nudged in the ribs by the girl sitting next to her.

"It's you, Karen," whispered the girl. "Go up to the front."

As Karen stepped forward, she was practically blinded by a camera flashbulb. She was trembling as she accepted the unexpected award. She managed to stammer a grateful, "Thank you very much."

She went back to her seat with the others and stared unbelievingly at the certificate she held in her hands.

Then the principal finished his "Farewell to Graduates," and Karen rose to make her response. Her knees felt like Jell-O. She wanted to run.

She stood in front of the microphone and waited for a moment, as she had been taught, to regain her composure. She took a deep breath and began, "If we had to condense everything we have learned during our four years of study at Marshall High School, each of us would have a different set of experiences to share, according to our own interests and participation. However, it is probable that many of us would have one thing in common. It would not be the memory of various facts of history or social studies, nor mathematical theorems, nor the English rules we might recall. It would be something derived from our classes in all these subjects." As Karen spoke, she gained confidence.

"It would be the mental attitude which our teachers helped us learn. They have provided us with principles to guide our creativity and confidence to use our new-found tools of learning. We realize that what we have constructed during our years at Marshall is a foundation on which we may build as we choose. Now, we're ready to take the next step. Some of us will be going immediately to join the work force, while others will be making further preparation for their life's work. What will determine the success or failure in our lives? To excel in a chosen field, to be a worthwhile individual, to live peacefully as a member of the family of man . . . much of this will be decided by what was done during the years here. Even though we say 'farewell,' we are not really ending our relationship with teachers and friends from Marshall. A part of Marshall will always be with us."

Karen moved across the stage to her place on a wave of applause. The group of seniors stood and the line started forward, one by one, as their names were called.

As she reached the back of the auditorium, Karen was immediately surrounded by a crowd of persons congratulating her on winning the scholarship and on her speech. Her head swam happily as she acknowledged all the well-wishers. At the same time, however, she looked hopefully around. She was certain that she would see her dad somewhere.

Karen continued to endure the handshaking and hugging along with directions to smile, while Mother and Gary took several snapshots of her with different groups of people.

As the crowd began to diminish, Mother said, "It's been a big evening. As the mother of the star of the show, I've got to go home and rest."

Karen continued to search the remaining faces in the auditorium. There was still no sight of Dad.

"Cliff, have you seen Dad anywhere? He wouldn't forget my graduation, would he?"

Before Cliff could answer, Mother said, "Perhaps something came up, and he felt he couldn't make the trip."

"He would have come no matter what," Karen insisted.

"This night is very special for you," Mother said. "We're not going to ruin it because one person didn't come. He had his reasons, I'm sure. Now, stand over there by Grandmother, and let me get one more picture of you. Then you and Gary can go on to the class party."

Submissively, Karen did as Mother directed, but she still continued to look about the empty auditorium. Why hadn't Dad come?

13.

A Step Forward

For the second time in one year, Karen found herself preparing for a major change in her life. This time, however, she had a feeling of permanency and a sense of direction. When she had moved from the family house on Linden Street last March, Mother had made her discard several things she wanted to keep. Now Karen found herself eliminating many of the remaining items that she once felt to be necessary to her happiness. She was aware that she could take only a limited number of possessions up to Northwood with her. Since Mother and Phil would be traveling in Mexico with a trailer, there would be no place for objects which weren't absolutely indispensable.

Mother and Phil had been home, following their wedding trip, for only a couple of days now, and both apartments were a confused jumble of the preparation to form one household where there had been two.

Karen decided to continue working at the Community Center Day Nursery right up to this last week before she would be leaving for college.

Late on a Friday afternoon she came home from work

tired and thoughtful. She got off the bus and walked slowly toward the apartment in the January darkness. Something Ray had suggested nagged at her consciousness.

"You've made an exceptional contribution to the children here at the nursery. You may have ability in the line of public service. Don't decide definitely on a journalism major until you've given yourself an opportunity to be certain where your real interests lie. Try some courses in education and sociology."

As Karen entered the apartment lobby, she saw a woman sitting on one of the chairs near the mailbox. The woman was sitting with her head resting on the back of the chair. Her eyes were closed.

Karen started to walk past her and then she stopped suddenly.

"Clara!" she exclaimed.

The woman sat up quickly and opened her eyes.

"I'm sorry," Karen apologized. "I didn't mean to startle you. I was only surprised to find you here."

"I wouldn't be here," Clara said, "if there had been any other way to contact you. I've written," Clara explained. "I tried to call you long distance last night, but you were out. I left a message with your mother to have you get in touch with me. When you hadn't returned my call by this morning, I decided that I'd drive down here and talk to you myself."

Clara appeared distraught. It confused Karen. She hadn't received any letters from the ranch for almost a month. Mother hadn't mentioned a phone call last night.

Clara eased her bulky form out of the chair. "We had an accident up at the ranch a few days ago. Your dad was loading some heavy saws on a truck. The boy who was helping him forgot to set the emergency brake. . . ."

"Is Dad all right?" Karen interrupted, anxiously. "He's not . . ."

Clara wiped her hand across her eyes. "He broke several ribs and two vertebrae. He's in the hospital, in traction. He has quite a bit of pain."

Clara's chin and lower lip trembled noticeably as she spoke, "Karen, I'm begging you. If you have any feeling for your dad, come back with me and see him. You can't imagine how hurt he has been, not hearing from you for so long."

"It seems that Dad has been too busy to think much about me," Karen replied angrily, feeling that she had been the one who was hurt by him. "He didn't even come to graduation."

"You made it very clear that you didn't want us at your graduation," Clara said. Her eyes were brilliant with angry tears now to match Karen's.

"What are you talking about?" Karen demanded.

"I'm talking about the letter that said you felt it would be embarrassing for you if we attended your graduation."

"I don't know what you're talking about."

"Please," Clara pleaded. "I didn't mean to start any unpleasantness. There has been enough of that already. All I wanted to do was to ask you to come north with me tonight. I know your dad would give anything in the world to see you and talk to you."

"I can't leave here right now," Karen said. She had to have time to understand what was happening. "Let me talk it over with Mother and I'll come if it can be worked out."

"I'm not going to leave here," Clara said firmly, "until I get an answer from you one way or another."

"I'll call you as soon as I can," Karen said, feeling uncomfortable under Clara's gaze. "Really I will. I promise."

She watched Clara leave the lobby of the apartment. Karen thought she seemed very weary and defeated. Karen wished she could have invited her upstairs to rest and eat something, but Karen was sure Mother wouldn't welcome Clara.

Karen remembered about the baby. Dad had said in his letter that Clara wasn't having an easy time of it. The long drive must have been an ordeal for her, possibly even dangerous. The roads weren't in very good condition this time of the year. Suddenly Karen didn't care what Mother would say, about Clara's being in the apartment. She rushed to the door of the apartment and ran out into the street.

"Clara," she called. "Clara?"

The streets were empty, except for a pair of red taillights blinking as they drove away.

Karen went back inside the building. She realized that Clara really cared for Dad. No, it was more than that. Karen had to be completely honest with herself. Clara obviously loved Dad very much.

Karen stood in the lonely lobby and looked out at the darkness. "I'm sorry," she whispered. "Forgive me, and take care of her. Please take care of her."

SLOWLY Karen walked up the three flights of stairs to the apartment. She was still puzzled by what Clara had said about having tried to get in touch with her. Mother hadn't mentioned any phone calls and there hadn't been any mail for her from the ranch for almost a month. A terrible suspicion was forming in the back of Karen's mind, but she didn't want to believe such a thing could be true.

Mother was busy in the kitchen. Karen could hear her rattling pots and pans about.

"Is that you, Karen?" she called. "Hurry and set the table. Phil will be home from work soon."

"Mother," Karen began. "Was there a long-distance telephone call for me last night?"

"How did you . . . ?" her mother asked in an alarmed tone. Then she regained control and said, "Yes, there was. I forgot to mention it."

"Has there been any mail for me lately that you've forgotten to give me?"

Her mother seemed to pale noticeably and said, "Karen, what's the matter with you?"

They stood facing each other uncomfortably with something unspoken hanging between them.

Finally Karen had to ask, "Mother, didn't it seem strange that Dad didn't come to my graduation?"

Mother bristled. "All right, Karen," she said. "We may as well quit hedging with each other. Evidently you know something or you're trying to find out something."

Karen wished with all her heart that this was only a bad dream.

"Yes, I wrote and suggested to your father that it might be the best thing for everyone concerned if he didn't attend the graduation ceremonies."

"You what?" Karen gasped.

"Now before you say anything we'll both regret, let me explain a few things you might not have considered. Your graduation was a night-of-nights for you. I wanted it to be perfect, something you'd always remember, something I never had. Because Phil is so fond of you, he went to a lot of trouble and expense to plan that lovely dinner party. It was only for family and close friends. You must admit it would have created a delicate situation to have had your father and his new wife along with us. It would have spoiled the fun completely. Then too, think how awkward it would have been for you to have had two sets of parents on hand to introduce to your classmates. I decided this was a much simpler solution. I was only thinking of your happiness."

Karen stared at Mother for a moment and then looked away. Mother really believed what she was saying! Karen was certain of that. How many times had Karen heard Mother and Dad excuse the things they did by saying, "I was only thinking of your happiness. . . . I was only doing what was best for you."

Karen was glad that Phil hadn't come home yet. She didn't think he knew what Mother had done.

Karen turned and left the kitchen.

"Where are you going?" Mother called.

"I'm going out for a walk," Karen said.

"So we're back to that," Mother snapped. "I hope that some day you'll learn that running away is no solution."

"I'm not running away," Karen said. "I want to think things over."

"I hope you do," Mother said. "I hope you give what I said a lot of thought."

Karen went out into the cold darkness. She walked for a few blocks and then turned toward the Humbolt Building. She took the elevator to the fifth floor. The receptionist at the desk at Station WXMW was closing the switchboard for the night.

"I beg your pardon," Karen said. "Is Mr. Harrison still here?"

The girl looked at her watch. "He's doing the six o'clock news," she said. "If you care to wait, he'll be out in a moment."

When Ray wheeled through the swinging studio doors,

Karen said, "I'm sorry to bother you at dinner time, Ray, but . . ."

For the next half hour Karen explained the situation to him. When she had given him all the facts, she said, "I can't understand some of the things my parents have done. My dad thought it would be best not to have me come up to the ranch at Christmastime. My mother decided that it would be best to write to Dad and tell him not to come to my graduation. They push and pull me, this way and that, until I'm nearly torn apart."

"Karen," Ray said reasonably. "Haven't you ever made an honest mistake in your life?"

"Of course I have." Karen wasn't sure what he was getting at.

"Are you perfect? Are you always good and kind and loving?"

"No," she replied, puzzled. "Nobody is perfect."

"Well, parents make mistakes, too. You've got to accept that. They make honest mistakes in judgment."

"But they ought to know better," she protested. "They're always telling me that their judgment is better than mine because they're older and they've had more experience than I have."

"Yes, parents ought to know better. Adults ought to be wise, but they're human beings with human limitations."

"They say that they want what is best for me. They say they love me," Karen cried out, "but they hurt me. Sometimes they hurt me so much I can hardly stand it."

"I know," Ray said, quietly. "They love you and yet they hurt you." He looked straight at her. "And it's possible that you hurt them, too, without ever intending to do so."

Karen sat helplessly and looked back at Ray's intent gaze. She knew what he had said was true. She had probably hurt them in a dozen ways that she couldn't even know about.

"I thought I had some answers," she said. "I really thought I could handle whatever problems came along, but this really set me back on my heels."

"Learning to cope with difficult situations is not something you can accomplish in one or two encounters. It's something you often have to learn all over again each time. It's a bit like climbing a rocky hillside. You struggle to take two steps forward and then you slide back one. It's maddening, but you have to remember that you did manage to take those steps, and you did advance one."

"Sometimes I think my biggest struggle is not so much learning to live with others as it is learning to live with myself," Karen admitted.

"That insight is worth several giant steps up the trail."

She smiled. "On up my two-way street. I guess that's the answer. I have to give as well as take. I'm going to miss you when I'm up at Northwood," Karen said.

"I'll miss you, too, Karen," he answered. "Because when a person tries to help a friend, he finds he has been assisted, too. And, Karen," he added. "Your mother and your dad need love, too."

"I'd better get home now," she said. "I've got lots to do if I'm going to catch a northbound train to Dad's tomorrow. And, . . ." she paused, feeling better than she had for a long time, "maybe I can get home in time to help Mother with the dishes."

Karen went out into the crisp winter air again. She didn't fool herself into thinking that she wouldn't have any more problems she couldn't handle. She knew she had a long way to go on this two-way street of life, this give-and-take. But it was good to be alive and have a chance.